The Bookbinder's Apprentice

and other

Impossible Love Stories

P.J. Braley

Spyglass Hill Press

Distributed by IngramSpark

Cover art by Freepik

To

Jack and Brenda

Books by P.J. Braley
and Between the Lines Publishing

The Fire Slayers
Finding Persephone
Persephone's Children

Table of Contents

On the Way to Elsa's Diner

"If you want a happy ending, that depends, of course, on
where you stop your story."
– Orson Welles

On the Way to Elsa's Diner

He told himself later that if he hadn't known her family, he would have let her find her own way. Or, if he had been thinking rationally, he would have realized that he didn't have time before catching the midnight train to Los Angeles to be her personal tour guide.

But he wasn't thinking rationally. Sitting alone in a corner booth where the morning's rays of filtered sunlight had not yet found him, he looked at the telegram one more time before slipping it into his coat pocket. He gave it a soft pat to confirm its existence and to make sure it would not slip away. He smiled and watched the smoke from his cigar curl upwards toward the ceiling. Life was finally opening up for him, and the future he had always dreamed of was becoming a reality. He had precious little time to lose. There were people to see, suitcases to pack, and the hotel needed to know where to forward his letters and messages.

Mentally rubbing his hands together in anticipation, he expected a great many messages now that the news that Hollywood had beckoned had spread throughout the backstages of Broadway. He had bided his time, watching as the film industry shifted from simple entertainment to a vehicle for social awareness and change. On the stage, he could only reach a thousand or fifteen hundred people at a time—and that was on a good night—and his radio work . . . well, he knew the limitations of that audience, but movies reached millions of people all over the globe. And he'd heard of a new invention called television that would put entertainment right in people's homes. His scope and his fame would know no boundaries. Nothing could stop him. It was 1939, and his time had arrived while he was still young enough, and arrogant enough, to claim it.

It was still early when he checked his watch. He had planned his last day in New York down to the minute, and it was time to get started. He was taking the last few draws from his cigar when a tentative creak from the hinges of the front door disturbed his thoughts, and, looking up, he saw her standing on the threshold of the diner. At first, she was nothing more than a delicate silhouette outlined by the pale morning light, but when she stepped into the diner, her shadowed beauty became a promise fulfilled. The luminosity of her eyes and the little-girl-lost look she had about her went straight to his heart, first cooling then stalling the fires of his ambitious itinerary.

"Excuse me, is this Elsa's Diner?" she asked with a soft southern drawl. She glanced slowly around the room as though looking for someone familiar. "My uncle owns it, and I was supposed to meet him there this morning."

"No," answered the waiter behind the counter. "Elsa's Diner is on *East* 48th Street. Not that I should be telling my customers about another diner, you understand."

"Which way?" she asked tentatively, the sparkle in her eyes faded in her confusion.

"I ain't no guide," the waiter said rudely. Seeing her forlorn expression, he started to apologize, "Well,—"

A deep voice emanated from the dimly lit corner.

"No, but I am," the actor said, putting out his cigar.

He stood up and threw his napkin on the table. The scene had unfolded in front of him like a badly rehearsed play, and he'd seen enough.

"Miss," he said, looking in her direction, "Allow me to escort you; it just so happens I'm going that way."

Within moments, he'd paid his bill, picked up her suitcase, and, with his free arm encircling her waist, whisked her back through the door and into the sunlight.

"If you will just point, sir, I can find it," she said, gently removing his arm.

"Although it is ungentlemanly to contradict a lady, Miss, you can't find it because if you could find it, you would already be there. You would never have walked into this diner in error, and I, therefore, would have forever missed the opportunity to be of service to you."

She didn't quite follow his logic but found the words, and the cadence of his voice, irresistible. Trying once more, she said, "But sir, I don't want to take up your time."

Time? Did he have the time? Mentally calculating the day, he estimated that this mission would only take fifteen to twenty minutes, and walking with her would be a very pleasant way to spend those minutes. He had the time, he had her attention, and the role of knight-in-shining-armor had always appealed to him. He smiled and, instead of encircling her waist, deferred to her modesty and offered her his arm. A very courtly gesture on his part, as became the proverbial knight, and she played along, curtseying before placing her white-gloved hand inside his elbow. And then she laughed.

That he was attracted to her was never in doubt. She was a damsel-in-distress who had brought her own light into the shadows of the diner. He knew as soon as he heard her voice that he was going to know her; it was a *fait accompli*. But when she laughed, he was smitten. He didn't want to be. There was no time in his life right now for such feelings. He tried to shrug them off and said, gruffer than he intended, "I know your aunt and uncle. Elsa and Arthur are friends of mine, and I wanted to see them before I left town. I said I was walking that way."

"Oh."

Her bright smile was only slightly subdued. "Well, you also said you were a guide, so please point out any places of special interest."

He stared at her. Her optimism floored him. Hadn't she looked around while she was searching for her uncle's restaurant? Places of interest? The Great Depression had decimated these neighborhoods. Interspersed with boarded-up shops were a few grocers with their smells, dusty pawnshops on every corner, hole-in-the-wall diners and saloons where you were never quite sure what you were eating—or drinking—and vacant lots where scruffy children played stickball among tin cans and empty bottles. Why, there wasn't even a decent theatre for at least another twelve blocks.

When she saw the look of incredulity on his face, she laughed again and tried to explain. "You see, I've never been to New York before, but I've dreamt about it all my life. I've seen it in movies and heard so many songs about New York that I keep expecting something wondrous around every corner."

Not around these corners, he thought. Suddenly, he could not bear the idea of anyone else showing her his favorite city. He knew, even though it was early, it would take all day just to see a few highlights, let alone the little treasures hidden here and there in the neighborhoods he frequented, and he also knew he did not have all day.

Deciding to shift the day's priorities a bit, he looked down at her and said, "Well, Miss, er, Bannister, is it?"

She hesitated. Regardless of how nice he seemed, he was still a stranger. She was in the big city now. She knew she had to be careful.

"Please, just call me Rose," she said shyly.

He caught the hesitation in her voice. "Is that your real name?"

"No, but it is my favorite flower, the small pink ones. Please, call me Rose; it is so much prettier than my real name."

"Ah," he said. A moment later, he recited, "What's in a name? That which we call a rose, by any other name, would smell as sweet."

"Oh, that was so nice," she said. "Did you just make that up?"

"No. I write . . . occasionally, but I didn't write that. It's from *Romeo and Juliet*." He could tell she did not recognize the name of the play. "By Shakespeare," he added.

She looked at him with new respect growing in her soft brown eyes. *Who was this person who could quote Shakespeare in the middle of such a dirty street?* She'd heard of Shakespeare, of course, and read some of his sonnets in the fifth form, but the school superintendent felt the plays were too worldly for young ladies.

"Do you know more?" she asked.

Now, it was his turn to laugh. "Hmm, just a little." Knowing he was blushing from ear to ear, he looked down at his feet. How refreshing. This girl did not know who he was. He could be anyone—or no one. For a little while, perhaps the entire morning, he preferred to be no one.

After reviewing his repertoire for a few moments, he snapped his fingers and smiled. "Somehow," he said, "I think these few lines were written just for you."

With hand over his heart like an old-time orator, he recited, "I know a bank where the wild thyme blows, where oxlips and the nodding violet grows, quite over-canopied with luscious woodbine, with sweet musk-roses, and with eglantine."

Her white gloves muffled her enthusiastic applause.

"That was wonderful!" she said. Then, tilting her head a bit, she asked, "What is eglantine?"

"Well, that's why it was written for you. Eglantine is a small pink rose."

Now, it was her turn to blush and look down. Sensing the importance of the day, she'd worn her best dress: a pink dotted

Swiss. Her eyes peeked out beneath her brown felt hat, decorated with the new pink ribbons she'd added for luck.

"You are so nice," she said, "with the Shakespeare and everything, but we really need to get to my uncle's restaurant. I left early so I would be there for the morning rush."

"My dear," he said, taking her hand, "it is really too late for that. Look around you; most people are at work now. The street is nearly empty."

To Rose's eyes, it looked as crowded as ever. "It is?"

"Yes. I'm afraid the best we will be able to manage is lunch. And," he returned her hand into the crook of his left arm, "if I have anything to say about it, we may not make it until dinner."

He picked up her suitcase, and together they walked toward Elsa's Diner. She noticed how the streets got cleaner as they walked uptown and, because she was looking for a restaurant, was surprised when they turned down a tree-lined street and stopped in front of a brown brick building.

"Just a minute," he said, turning a brass knob. Winking at her, he added, "Let me do the talking."

She heard a ringing inside the house, and the door opened.

"Good morning, Miss Maisie," he said to the woman standing in the doorway. "Arthur and Elsa are expecting this young lady today—their niece. Please send one of the boys around to the restaurant to tell them she's with me, and I promise to bring her to the diner later this afternoon. I am showing her the town."

Maisie eyed the girl up and down. "Humph, they aren't going to like that. She was supposed to start work this morning. And they sure aren't going to like that *you* are showing her the town. I heard about what happened last time. Why, it was in all the pa—"

Before Maisie could finish, his well-trained voice drowned out her last few words.

"You mustn't believe everything you read, Miss Maisie, and I promise to return her as good as new. In the meantime, here is her suitcase," he said, placing it inside the vestibule.

With her hands on her hips, Maisie looked disapprovingly at them both.

"As good as new?" Rose asked with a grin as they turned and walked away. "What was that all about?"

"It was about nothing," he said a little too loudly, tossing the words over his shoulder. "Some people just don't have enough to do."

When the door slammed, they laughed and, like truant children afraid of being caught, hurried down the street.

Stopping at the corner to catch their breath, she asked him his name. He paused for a moment. She may not recognize his face, but she might recognize his name, and perhaps she, too, had read something scandalous . . . .

"You can call me George."

"Is that your real name," she teased him, "or is George the name of your favorite president?"

"George is my real name." It was true, but no one had ever called him George except his mother.

"And though," he said, "it cannot be denied that George Washington was a great president, the fact is I was named after my mother's father."

"And," she said laughing, "I suppose you cannot tell a lie."

"Oh, no," he said, looking deeply into her eyes and, using his *Othello* voice, added, "I can lie." Her smile disappeared from her face like the sun hides behind a cloud. She pulled her hand away and stepped back. Normally, he would reward himself for manipulating his audience so deftly, but he panicked. *What if she ran back to the house?* He could lose her.

"But not today," he said softly, "and Rose, I promise, I'll never lie to you."

Responding to the sincerity in his voice, she put her hand back on his arm.

"Well, George, where do we go from here?"

His eyes swept the street and looked back into her upturned face.

"We'll go wherever you wish, my dear."

And they did.

They strolled up streets and down avenues. Sometimes, he hailed a taxi, sometimes they jumped on a streetcar, but mostly they walked. She didn't want to miss anything. And, as they walked, she told him what it was like growing up in a small town in Virginia, and he told her stories about New York. It was home to him, but to her, it was the most exotic, fascinating place she had ever seen. She loved the dirty children and smiled at the street vendors. He pointed out important buildings and landmarks. She surprised him with her intelligence and charmed him with her innocence. He bought her a hotdog with sauerkraut and watched as her nose wrinkled at the smell and how her eyes widened when she discovered how much she liked it.

He could have taken her to any fancy restaurant in town. He knew them all—but they knew him—and he did not wish to be known. On that day, he was just George, a friend of her uncle's. It was a very tenuous role he was playing, and because it was important that no one destroy the illusion, he completely avoided the theatre district. She didn't know the difference. He had never seen anyone so happy with so little of him. Everyone else wanted the "Great Shakespearean Actor." She didn't even know that man existed.

That anonymity was important, but at the same time, he wanted her to know everything about him. He was tempted to take his ticket for one to LA and exchange it for two, but thought it best if they waited until after he was settled and came back for her. He knew he was being impulsive, but it was part of what made him a great actor. His most memorable performances were not characterizations developed over time but those based on the spontaneity of his insight. That insight had carried him from Kenosha, Wisconsin, to New York City, and although he had visited Los Angeles and Hollywood, neither of them could compare to the Great White Way of Broadway for prestige. Once again, he decided to trust his instincts. His only concern was what he would do if she did not want to accompany him. It was a question of whether she *wanted* to be with him that would tip the scales in his favor. Knowing their future depended on the answer to that question, he became the best George in his repertoire. He played the roles of a knight, a gentleman, a father, and a brother, and when she exclaimed over a box of puppies in a store window, he went in and promptly bought her one, the little white one with a pink collar and leash.

"Oh, no, George," she said, cradling the puppy. "You mustn't spend your money like this."

The heartfelt gratitude in her eyes made him feel like a millionaire. "I want you to have her," he said, smiling, "to keep you company. I have to leave tonight to take care of some business in California."

"I'll keep her only if you promise to come back," she said, burying her nose in the dog's fur.

For the first time, he took her in his arms.

"I'll be back, Rose," he said, not bothering to disguise the deep rumble of sensuality in his voice.

His lips barely brushed her forehead before she eased out of his embrace.

Afraid of what he would see in her eyes, she did not look up. "Of course, George, you have to come back. I don't think we've seen *everything* yet."

"You are right, my dear, and since we have a dog now, we must go to the park. It's where all the best dogs go." He held her hand, she held the leash, and they looked, for all the world to see, like two people who had known each other forever.

Unwilling to conclude their journey too quickly, he took the long way to the park. The dog, being new to a leash and wanting to go this way and that, tugged at it constantly. Soon realizing the dog was too much of a distraction, George regretted his impulse to buy it for her.

Sensing his discomfort, Rose said, "It means so much to me to have something to hold on to, George. Really, I can't thank you enough. I thought I was going to be so homesick, but now I won't feel that way. I just hope Uncle Arthur and Aunt Elsa don't mind another mouth to feed. But I suppose I can save Tina some scraps from the diner."

"Who is Tina?"

"This is Tina," she said, gesturing to the leash. "For Eglantine."

"You remembered."

"I don't think I'll ever forget anything about today," she said, smiling.

"Nor will I."

The trees of the park were just ahead when they passed a photography studio. The gilded sign in the window read "Photographs While You Wait—One Dollar."

It was all the money she had.

"Oh, George, let's get our picture taken. I have a dollar, and that way, I'll have your picture *and* Tina to keep me company while you're away."

He didn't want his picture taken. He knew there was a good chance the photographer would recognize him, and it would spoil the day.

"Just you," he said.

"And Tina?"

"And Tina," he agreed, taking a dollar from his wallet. "And I'll pay. This one is for me. You keep your money until next time."

He lit a cigar and stood outside the studio, paced a bit, and, pulling down his hat, browsed the used bookstore next door. By the time he had come to the end of his cigar, she was back, excited and beaming.

"Look, George. It's both of us!"

He gazed at the beautifully hand-tinted photograph. Rose, her eyes bright and smiling happily, sat in a white wicker chair with Tina next to her. *This,* he thought, *is what I want. I could be happy.*

"Put it in your pocket," she said, "so you won't forget us."

"I would sooner forget my own name," he said, sliding the photograph into his pocket. Smiling and confident, he slipped her hand through his arm and held it there.

Entering the park, Rose was amazed. One moment, she was in a big, noisy city, and the next, a cool, shaded forest. It seemed just like home. The trees muffled the sounds of the traffic and hid the gray buildings. She could almost believe she'd imagined it all. Halfway through the park, they stopped at the fountain so she could give the dog a drink of water. Laughing, she splashed a little on her face.

"Oh," she said, picking up her gloves, "I left my hankies in my suitcase."

"Let me," he said, patting the drops from her face with his handkerchief. "See, just as I promised, 'good as new.'"

She smiled into his eyes. She trusted him now, and he could feel it. He also felt that he could tell her anything . . . anything, but who he was. So, he talked of his boyhood and his college friends, the books he had read and the movies he liked, all the while carefully omitting the details of his immediate future. She listened as he spoke. Nodding and smiling, she believed every word he said.

The shade of the trees grew deeper, and the sunlit spots were rarer. It was getting late. Walking back toward town, they shared a bag of peanuts he'd bought from a street vendor: one peanut for him, one for her, and half of one for the dog. They stopped at the edge of the park—he wanted to ask her something—but whether it was meaningful or just about who got the next peanut, he never quite remembered. All he was able to recall was when he looked down at her, their eyes met, and, for that moment, nothing else existed. He dropped the nearly empty bag, she let go of the leash, and the universe revolved around them in complete silence.

The sharp sound of a car horn and the yelp of a dog pierced their world. Suddenly, she became aware that the leash was no longer in her hand. Her eyes frantically searched the street as she dashed heedlessly in the direction of the dog's cry. He, who was usually so quick, took a full half minute to realize that she was no longer standing in front of him. Thirty seconds of realization— one lifetime of trying to forget.

When the police arrived, they wrote down the names and addresses of the witnesses. One police officer noticed him standing where she'd left him. Believing he might be a witness, the officer walked up to him.

"Did you see it happen?"

"No," he said, "just the result."

A throng of reporters descended on the scene. He turned away and once again pulled his hat over his eyes. The officer was not used to being ignored and looked suspiciously into the man's face. He became instantly solicitous.

"Oh, Mr. We—"

"Please, no names. Reporters . . . ."

"Oh," the officer whispered conspiratorially, "was she a friend of yours? Maybe you should sit down. Can I call someone?"

"No, I must catch a train to Los Angeles this evening; there are people I have to see. I, I need to pack and leave forwarding addresses." He answered the officer's questions as though reading a script, but his voice grew stronger as he returned from the fog of the last few minutes.

"Did you know her?"

"Only slightly. She's the niece of Arthur Bannister, the guy who owns Elsa's Diner on East 48th Street."

"I know the place. What's her name?"

"I'm not sure. I just met her today, her first day in New York. She asked me to call her Rose because it was her favorite flower," he said. Then, almost to himself, he whispered, "Just a little bud of a rose."

He had to leave. "Do you need me to stay? I didn't see it happen; I was standing here waiting for her to come back so I could show her the way to her uncle's restaurant."

He would never go there now; he could not be involved. Arthur may never forgive him for not taking better care of his niece, but he would despise him if his reputation turned a family tragedy into a citywide scandal. The papers, he knew from recent experience, would tear her to pieces. Using all his acting skills to conceal the panic he felt, he awaited the officer's reply.

"Naw, just looks like one of those things, a typical accident. Kinda sad, though, so young, what, eighteen, nineteen? Out-of-towners just don't understand the traffic here. We'll contact her relatives."

The police officer turned away, muttering to himself, "Chasing dogs in the middle of the street like it was a country road . . . and, of course, the dog gets away, but her—" he sighed and shook his head. Glancing back, he said, "Thank you for your help, sir. You can go."

Go? Go where? Oh, yes, to the hotel, to pack, to use his ticket for one to California. He checked the coat pocket containing his ticket to give him a sense of reality and felt something else. Reaching into the pocket, he removed a photograph of a girl and a dog. There was so little light left he could barely see her—but he saw the dog. The anger that would one day become legendary welled up in him. He tore the photograph in half and crushed the dog's picture under his heel. He put her half back in his pocket and, in the fading light, walked away from the park, the crowd, the reporters, and the pink dress that looked like a rag in the street.

When he returned to the hotel, the sun had completely gone down. He went through the motions of leaving one town for another. Packing quickly, he returned a few telephone calls, but most of the eagerly anticipated messages were thrust unread into his pocket.

Leaning against the balcony rail of the smoking car of the train speeding westward, he lit a cigar. He pulled the messages from his coat and read them in the lamplight. He smiled at most, frowned at some, and threw them away. Thinking he had come to the last one, he saw it wasn't a message, but the torn photograph. He stared at it until the crosswind from a passing train ripped it from his hand. He made no effort to retrieve it. He did not even turn his head but stared down at his empty fist.

For years, he looked for her around every corner. When he couldn't find her, he tried to invent her, but her innate innocence eluded him. He married other women, beautiful women, but he did not love them, and when the glamour wore off, they left him.

In the days before he died, the housekeeper saw him wandering from room to room, looking through old boxes of awards, clippings, scripts, and letters. "Where is she?" he asked each time he opened another box. Whenever he found a woman's photograph, he held it in his fist and stared at it, thinking that if he looked long enough, it would become her face, hand-tinted and delicate.

He just wanted to see her once again, but with all his imagination and desire, he could not make that wish come true. Refusing to become a caricature of his own creation, he died slumped over his typewriter, soundlessly and alone.

Something lightly touched his arm. He looked down at a small white glove.

A soft, southern voice recited, "I know a bank where the wild thyme blows and the nodding violet grows."

He looked up. It was her smile and her eyes. The pink ribbons of her hat and her pink dress swayed gently in the mist.

On the strength of her small, gloved hand, he stood up. "Can we go there?" he asked.

She tucked her hand into the crook of his arm.

"We'll go wherever you wish, my dear."

And they did.

The End

A Small Fire

"There are some people who live in a dream world,
and there are some who face reality,
and then there are those who turn one into the other."
– Desiderius Erasmus

A Small Fire

I scarcely noticed the yellow flowers dancing to the music of the summer breeze as I hurried toward the house where my research subject had once lived. Half doctoral investigation—half labor of love, I finally had a chance to see the chambers he inhabited, the carpets he walked, and the table where he wrote.

Scheduling an appointment with a historian to view the interior had been difficult. Every email I received advised me that the five-hundred-year-old house was currently under restoration and closed to the public. It had taken all my powers of persuasion, writing skills, months of networking, and, in some cases, downright bribery until the friend of a friend acquiesced to arranging an interview and private tour. Receiving notice of the invitation on the final day of my research trip to Basel, Switzerland, I had only hours to spare before boarding the last train for Amsterdam. With my ticket in my pocket and my bags checked at the station, I planned to spend as much time as possible discussing not only the residence but also the man who was a monk, priest, scholar, humanist, and writer that history still remembers as the heart, soul, and pen of the European Renaissance during the 15th and 16th centuries. There was so much to learn, and I had walked so swiftly most of the way, that I was gasping for breath when I found the house.

I knew European social customs frowned severely on arriving early, but my time was short. However, despite my determination, I slowed down as I approached the three-storied white house. Encouraged by the freshly painted shutters and colorful trim around the doors, I hoped someday it would be restored as magnificently as he deserved. Looking more like a tourist than a graduate student, I was taking some photographs of the house for my files when a young man waved from the gate.

"Hallo! Are you Katherine Egan?"

"Yes, are you Marcus?"

He nodded, and I met him at the gate. After I entered, he locked it behind us, then led me down a short walk to the side door.

"If the docent isn't already here," he said, "she will arrive in a few minutes."

"That's okay. I don't mind waiting, I know I'm early. I'll just take a few photographs. It's a dream come true, you know, just to be here. Thank you so much for everything you've done."

"It wasn't me," he said, "I am just helping a friend." He glanced at his watch. "Will you be staying long, Miss Egan?"

"Oh, please call me Kate. Uh, no, I can't. I have a ticket for the evening train to Amsterdam."

"Amsterdam? More research?"

"Always more research."

He smiled understandingly and held the door as I entered the house.

"Wait for the docent, Kate," he admonished. "This house is centuries old. It might look sturdy, but right now most of that is cheap plaster and paint, so don't go wandering."

"I'll wait," I promised.

"I'm locking the outside door. We don't want people just walking in. This isn't a tourist attraction . . . yet."

Without another word, he closed the door, and I heard the key twist in the lock.

Sitting in the small anteroom, I looked at my cellphone and checked the time on my itinerary. I tried not to be anxious, but every minute I spent alone was one less minute I could ask questions. I mentally reviewed my interview outline. Confident I would get answers to all my most important questions, I checked my phone again.

Damn, the battery was getting low. I looked around for an outlet, then remembered the charger was in my suitcase. At the station.

The minutes crawled by.

I tapped my phone again. The docent was nearly half an hour late.

The red "charge me" icon pulsated, and I became jealous of every moment slipping away. Glancing down the dark, empty hall, it occurred to me that she might be working in her office and had lost track of time, or perhaps she arrived at another entrance and was unaware of my presence. What if she were tapping her phone impatiently while waiting for me?

I had spent months planning and preparing for this interview, and I wasn't going to leave without it. Despite Marcus's warning, I decided to look for her.

Heavily shaded sconces lit the partially furnished rooms as I made my way through the large house. Investigating the layout of the first floor, it was clear that any recent renovations had been limited to refurbishing the impressive front library. Once past the gleam of glass and smell of leatherbound books, I navigated around the canvas drop cloths and paint cans that explained the partially painted and bare walls.

Walking from one hall to another, I called out as I knocked on each door. The uneven floors creaked and groaned beneath my feet, and many doors were locked or opened into empty, cobwebby rooms. Instead of the partially restored beauty that I expected, I was distressed by the evident lack of care for the house and its general shabbiness. Disappointed with what I had seen so far, I gave up on the tour. I just wanted to get the interview and leave.

At the end of the corridor on the second floor, a sign with a single word written in capital letters in a language I didn't understand was tacked to a door. American-born and fluent in

Latin, Dutch, and French, I guessed the word was either from a German or an Alemannic dialect. Hoping it translated as "office," I typed the word into my phone and impatiently scrolled down the list of translated words. Then I stopped. The word wasn't Northern European, nor was it "office." It was my name. In Greek.

Smiling, I opened the door and stepped into the room.

I was startled by the silence. Sunbeams cutting through broken shutters illuminated a jumble of furniture and yellowed stacks of papers tied with string. Spellbound by the play of dust motes swirling in the light and the sheer timelessness of the room, several moments passed before I realized I must have mistyped the word into the translator app. This wasn't anyone's office. I started backing out of the room when a movement near the window caught my eye.

Nearly hidden behind faded curtains, a young woman dressed in period costume turned in my direction. Tall and blond, her wide blue eyes tilted slightly above prominent cheekbones.

Unsure why she would be in a room with my name on it, I said, "Hello, are you the docent? Someone was going to tell me about the house."

Stepping toward me, she smiled and asked, "In English?"

"Yes, please."

She nodded, and instead of sitting in the chair behind the desk, she moved the curtain behind her and sat primly on the window seat. Pointing to a boudoir chair in the center of the room, she said, "Please make yourself comfortable."

Immediately charmed by her Renaissance-era dress and relieved to have found my guide, I resisted the impulse to brush the dust off the chair before sitting down. I took out my phone to record the interview, but realized the battery would never last long enough. Returning it to my bookbag, I removed my research folder. Surreptitiously glancing around as I opened my notebook, I realized the only items in the room not covered with dust were the printed emails and letters scattered on the table that I instantly recognized as my own. Obviously more storeroom than office, I knew there had to be better places in the house to stage an interview.

"Why are we meeting in here?"

"My story begins here."

"Is your story about him?" I asked, indicating an old postcard of one of his Holbein portraits thumbtacked to the wall above the table.

"Yes," she said.

"That's great! It's why I'm here—to learn more."

"Yes, I'm aware of why you're here. You were very persuasive, and, of course, he always had a fondness for students."

"Is it a long story?"

"This is *your* interview," she said, "the ending is not always up to me, but the story will explain our presence in this room and, perhaps, answer most of your questions."

She leaned against the back of the chair. Looking out the window, she closed her eyes against the harsh sunlight. My carefully memorized research outline vanished from my thoughts. I was enchanted by her loveliness, the beauty of her high-waisted brocade gown, and the sheerness of the kirtle she wore underneath. Listening to her lilting voice, I became caught up in her story like a rapt schoolgirl.

"It is always mid-winter in my memories," she began. "The moonlight shines through the window, creating a rainbow of frosted lace on the glass. The dulled echoes of the clock striking its vibrating strokes of ten, eleven, and twelve have died away, and I know I will not have to wait much longer. Staring at the ceiling, I listen . . . and pray.

"I track his footsteps as he paces in the chamber above me. Back and forth, pause, then back and forth again. He is worried because there is so much to do, to think, to write—letters, essays, translations, travel plans, but no, probably not travel plans. Age has not been kind to him, and he doesn't travel as often anymore. Those who wish to see him must come here."

Expecting a pause so I could ask a question, I was surprised when she continued without a glance in my direction.

"When the moon rises, the window darkens, and his footsteps cease. My hands tremble, and I can barely breathe for listening. He taps his walking stick softly on the tapestried floor. Once. Twice. Not loud enough to wake me if I am sleeping, and far too soft for anyone else to hear who is not listening for its whispered plea. Easing from my warm nest, I quickly wrap myself in a thick grey robe and pull on short lambswool stockings to keep my feet warm and my footsteps silent.

"I do not need a lamp to walk through the shadowy halls that I know well by day. Without a stumble, I climb the winding back staircase. Without hope, I say a prayer at his door, and without knocking, I enter the room.

"'Hurry, girl!' he says, trying to keep his voice low. The attempt makes me smile. It is difficult for him because he does not possess a quiet voice. Once heard in the courts of kings and cathedrals of popes, his is a voice that was never meant for intrigue. Still, he tries."

She laughed softly to herself as though she could still hear his whispery voice.

"And he must try . . . for I am a secret, though not his first secret because he does not trust easily, but I may be his last and, by far, the least important."

"He is waiting for me, and I can almost see the coverlets tremble. Stepping to the side of the bed, I toss my robe over the embroidered eiderdowns covering his long, lean frame and quickly slide next to him. Impatiently, he pulls my gown over my head.

"'You're warmer without it,' he says, enveloping me with his arms, his legs twist tightly around my own—"

"Wait a minute," I said, interrupting her. "I'm not sure I need to hear any more,"

I simply did not care for the direction this "interview" was taking. I didn't need to know his private life—and indeed, unsubstantiated, sensationalist fiction was the last thing I wanted in my dissertation. It was a waste of my time.

As though awakened from a dream, she opened her eyes slowly and looked directly into mine.

"You are a scholar," she said, "and all you know about him is from books. If you had found everything you needed, you would not have come here. Never forget that the only reason I am here is at your request to take you beyond those limitations. Therefore, I must ask that you not interrupt me again. You may, of course, leave at any time."

Unsure of where her story would lead but aware that we had not touched on any of my interview questions, I said, "You surprised me, that's all. I don't want to leave . . . yet."

She smiled at my hesitation. Then, once again leaning back and closing her eyes, she continued, her voice exactly the same as though I had never spoken.

"There is no intimacy in his voice, and I do not know if his words are spoken through lips soft or stern. No curiosity directs his fingers as they hug my softness against his chest. There is no suggestiveness in the way his hips press against mine. No desire stirs the weight of his maleness resting unapologetically against my thigh.

"Despite the wrapped hearthstones at his feet, his bed is cold. My heat slowly steals into his body, melting the tension of his muscles. His grip eases, and I can breathe deeply again. Warmed and supine, his breathing becomes rhythmic, soft, and steady. A lullaby of whispered cadences of prayers and songs in languages

I do not understand quiet my sensibilities, too, and my eyes grow heavy and close."

As though actually resting, her recitation slowed, and she took several soft breaths before starting again.

"Our nights are unremarkable, and we usually sleep undisturbed, but one night, he woke me laughing. I had never before heard him laugh. It was such a young, sweet sound that it almost broke my heart—and I envied him his dream. My dreams are not as joyful. As chaste as when I first entered his house, there is no wantonness in our relationship. I am not his wife, his mistress, or concubine, for he will have none of these. He says I am his *kleine vuur*—small fire. It's a lovely metaphor, but I have no need of linguistic illusions to disguise the truth."

I had to stop her again. "What do you mean?" I asked.

She blushed when she looked at me, then dropped her eyes. "I, I am little more than his warming cushion," she said.

"Wait. What? I'm sorry to interrupt, but are you saying you were hired to keep him warm at night?"

She laughed softly and shook her head.

"No, I came to work here as a scribe. We submit samples of our copy work, and he hires scribes as he needs them. He did not even know I was a woman until I arrived, and instead of dismissing me, he insisted I have a chamber to myself."

I looked around me. "This room?"

"Yes, it once had a simplicity that was quite lovely." She felt the flimsy curtain, sighed, and wiped her fingers on her skirt.

"Then, how did it happen?" I asked.

"I grew curious after several nights of listening to someone restlessly pacing on the third floor. First, I asked who occupied the room on the floor above me. Then, I asked why he could not sleep. Although I didn't know how to help—especially after I learned whose chamber it was—his restless pacing soon felt like footsteps on my heart. One night, I thought of a way, and the next time we were alone in the small scriptorium, I suggested bundling. It is quite common in the north. He shook his head and said we must not speak of such things, but after an especially brutally cold night, he gratefully accepted. A promise was made, and he kept it.

"All the other scribes are gone now, but he wants me to stay. He says I am useful to him. Because he is often misquoted, sometimes accidentally, sometimes maliciously, he keeps copies of everything he writes. By sunlight and lamplight, I copy the letters he sends all over Europe and the manuscripts he sends to his publishers. By moonlight, I shield him from the shards of the relentless winter wind that seek to steal his sleep, chill, and sicken him."

Although I did not want to interrupt her again, seeds of incredulity had taken root in my mind. I knew that, from the beginning of recorded history to the experiences in my own life, men did not always keep their promises—not even the best of them, and although this was not the interview I had prepared for or could have ever anticipated, I had to ask the most fundamental question.

"You are a beautiful woman. How was such an arrangement possible? At some point, surely, he must have wanted . . . well, you know . . . more." I tried to keep skepticism from showing on my face, but she must have heard it in my voice and did not speak for several moments.

"I understand what you are asking. There was 'more' in my life," she said, "before I came here. I was abandoned at a convent as a small child. As soon as I could hold a pen, I was taken to their scriptorium and learned to form letters before I learned to read them. I became quite adept at copying, and I was pushed to do more and more work, but when I cried that my hand hurt, I was punished. I ran away to what I hoped would be freedom, but I didn't realize how sheltered I had been and found I had traded one kind of imprisonment for another—one where 'more' was the only coin a woman owned. Then I heard about this monk, a scholar, who needed scribes, and I had nothing to lose. I didn't trust it at first. Every deception begins with a kind voice, but I soon learned that such desire matters little in a house such as this, and I was grateful."

Her voice dropped off at the end, and I realized that I was not only captivated by her story—I was also beginning to believe it.

Sighing and clasping her hands in her lap, she looked at me with eyes full of contrition and regret. I felt a catch in my throat and braced myself for the revelation that the writer I revered most in all Christendom had feet of clay.

"He broke his promise," I whispered.

She took a deep, shuddering breath.

"One night, roused by a branch brushing against his window, I awoke to find our usual positions reversed. Embracing him from behind, my hands met over his chest, my leg crossed over his. I was not fully awake, or I would have never dared, as I did then, to press my lips against his bare shoulder. I will never forget the feel of his skin, dry and smooth, the fragrance of smoky embers, and the taste of lavender. The sweetest moment of my memory lasted less than the time it takes to say the words. When he began turning slowly in my arms, I realized he was awake, and fear gripped my heart. You see, I had broken *my* promise."

She hesitated, brushing her hands over her face as though the memory hurt her. "There was no anger in his voice, only patience. He lifted my chin and looked into my eyes. 'That was very nice, but never again,' he said quietly, 'never again.' Shy and ashamed, I moved away from him, but he gathered me close, 'Don't cry, child,' he said, 'rest. Just lie still and rest so that we might renew our strength for the tasks of the day ahead. That is what the night is for.'"

She looked up at me with a glimmer of defiance. "I am not now, nor was I then, a child, but it was how he saw me. This unwavering perspective created an insurmountable wall of mutual trust in whose shadow we slept without lust, without sin, and without . . . love."

She smiled to herself.

"I told him once that if he should ever not need me, I would return to the convent, and he said, 'No child, you must marry. Our Blessed Father only requires that you give Him your soul; the life He gave to you should remain your own.'"

"I laughed at the time and told him, 'Perhaps that is true, but God seems to have forgotten my dowry.' He answered, not unkindly, 'It is well then that you have a fine hand for copy work because, without a dowry, not even the nuns will take you back.'

"He was right about that, but then, Desiderius was right about most things."

"You called him 'Desiderius'?"

"Not then, but he's dead now, and he doesn't mind."

She looked out the window, and I sensed her portrayal was ending. I glanced down at my watch. I still had time. Even if I had to run to the station, there was no way I was leaving before she finished her story.

"How did you manage not to get caught?"

She looked at the tattered postcard on the wall and tilted her head as though remembering her lines.

"Always rising before dawn for prayers, he doesn't wake me or ask me to leave. He doesn't have to. Attuned to his every movement and sound, I am already pulling on my gown before he has found his slippers. Gathering my robe, I quickly run down the dark stairs and fall into my cold bed. Huddled in the robe that carries the scent and warmth of his chamber, I sleep until the morning bells.

"He knows it would be worse for me than him if I am discovered, and so he is grateful, if not generous. I have no special place in his house—or his heart. I am only a means to an end. He

31

knows he cannot write if he does not sleep, and he cannot sleep if he is cold and shivery. And he must write; it is the air to him. There are times when I think his writing is the only thing that makes him feel that the world will not forget him."

"And it never has," I said. Hoping to keep the charade going for a little longer, I added, "But the world knows nothing of you."

"I am no one. Evidence of my existence hangs solely upon these words, but being part of *that* work, *that* life as a fire—however small—has come to me as a quiet happiness. Therefore, I keep our secret and insist that you keep it as well and protect my story: the unconsecrated confession of a passion that could never be spoken and would never be shared. It is a disciplined life within his shadow and a fine line to walk, but it has made me strong. And, if dwelling in silence is the only way I am allowed to love him—or to remain a part of his life—it is enough, isn't it? Isn't it?"

Feeling pressed for a response, for validation, perhaps even for absolution, I realized I was now part of her performance with lines of my own, and I answered her with my whole heart, "Yes. Yes, I believe it is."

But my response did not ease the tension in the room. After several moments of silence, I said, "So, you loved him." It was a statement, not a question.

"So," she repeated quietly to herself, "I loved him." Looking pleadingly up at me, she said, "You have read his words and loved him. Imagine then, seeing his struggle to be understood, to inspire change, to know his strength, and his frailty—how could you live in that shadow, day and night, and not love him?"

"You couldn't." My eyes shone with an admiration that was part envy. *Yes, she was right. To be a part of that life . . . of that work—no, his life, his work—would be worth almost any sacrifice.*

"A legend doesn't become a legend alone," I said. "That is the thesis of my dissertation, you know. There are always those who history does not name who made that distinction inevitable."

I hesitated for a moment. "I'm not sure how much of your story will go into my paper, but the afternoon has been unforgettable."

She smiled and leaned back into the chair. Glancing out of the window, she said softly, "So many things I'll never forget. Even the saddest day is embedded forever in my memory."

"Were you with him when he died?"

"No, I could not go to him when he was ill. Each time, I was afraid I would never see him again, but he reminded me that great men—even those who outlive their greatness—are not permitted to die unwitnessed. I prayed during the day as I copied his words, and I prayed at night as I listened to the murmurs and scuffle of other feet above my head while waiting for a summons that never came."

She blinked rapidly and, as though on cue, a single tear fell upon her pale cheek. I thought at first it was a bit of a cliché, too predictable to be real, but I found myself tearing up as well.

"Death did not take him by surprise," she said briefly. "Nothing did.

"He left me a little money, a dowry of sorts, giving me the luxury of choice. I followed his advice and chose to be married, and I have learned that the night is for many things, rest being just one of them. And so," she sighed, looking once again at his photograph, "in gratitude for his giving me the chance to choose a different life, I keep him alive in memory and conceal the truth."

"Why, then," I asked, deciding to play along with her desire to be treated as a wraith, "when you obviously had a full life beyond these walls, do you linger here?"

Expecting an eloquent denouement, I was surprised to see that when she turned back to me, all of the serenity had left her face.

"Why, then, do you linger here?" she demanded, pointing to my messages and letters. "When you could learn more about him almost anywhere else in the world, why did you attempt to move heaven and earth so you could be in this house on this day?

"This day?"

"It is the anniversary of his death," she said. Her hand clutched at her heart. "Have you no mercy?"

Too stunned to respond right away, I was greatly relieved when her soft smile returned, and she fell back into her gentle reminiscence.

"You don't have to answer. I know why. It is his way. Popes and kings, priests and princes, women, and men . . . not even Martin Luther could resist him. He was not without faults—he could not help being who and what he was—but their constant criticism and demands eventually tore him to pieces until he no longer had the strength to gather himself together. I would hate them if I could, but he did not, and so, I must not."

"I understand."

Her eyes narrowed, and she stood up quickly.

"*Do you?*" she asked accusingly.

Before I could answer, she held up her hand. A light came to her eyes, and a secret played upon her lips as she inclined her head. Looking up, she nodded. Once. Twice.

Watching her face and so caught up in the imagery and drama of her life, I thought I heard two soft raps. I glanced upward, expecting to see the vaults of heaven, but there was only a water-stained ceiling pockmarked with jagged craters from fallen plaster.

Disappointed and slightly embarrassed, I looked back toward the window.

She was gone.

I stood up so quickly that my chair tipped over. I turned and fled the room. Running toward the staircase, the staccato sounds of my shoes on the bare floorboards echoed throughout the house. Focusing on the rooms above me, I pulled the yellow tape away from the banisters and raced up the spongy steps that crumbled, split, and collapsed beneath my feet.

***

The curtains trembled as Clarisse tried to hide her laughter as she pressed the numbers on her cell phone.

"Marcus, she's on her way down. She totally bought it. You should have seen her! She bolted out of here like a shot. I'll grab her bag and meet you both downstairs. Americans can be so gulli—wait! What was that?"

"It sounded like a scream from inside the house."

"Has she come down?"

"Not yet."

Clarisse ran from the room and stopped when she saw the yellow tape, torn and coiling across the floor. In the sudden silence, she moved closer and saw the stairsteps, splintered and broken.

"Marcus, call . . . call an ambulance."

***

The new carpet muffles the sound of my footsteps as I pass refinished walls and colorful tapestries gleaming in the lamplight. My heart soars at the beautiful restoration. *Of course!* The renovation began on the top floor, which explains why the downstairs was still unfinished.

Hesitating before the entrance to his room, I see a small sign nailed to the door. Handwritten in small, neat letters, the words **"Do Not Disturb"** are repeated in several languages, but what care have I for signs? I was invited here.

Expecting it to be locked, I twist the iron L-shaped handle and press hard against the door.

The cold metal turns so easily that my hand slips, and I stumble over the threshold. Regaining my footing, I stand up slowly as the door closes behind me on silent hinges. The scent of wood smoke and lavender surrounds me like the blurred edges of a dream. As reverent as though I were entering a church, I step up into a large dark chamber warmed only by the dying embers of a small fire.

I am here. In his room. Standing on the floor upon which he walked. Next to the fireplace is the table where he wrote. Neatly stacked parchment gleams in the smoldering glow of a guttering candle. Fighting the urge to laugh in complete happiness, I walk toward his desk. I yearn to touch it, to run my hands lightly over the surface like found treasure. I want to create a memory that will last the rest of my life.

Before taking another step, a chill of air drifts through the room, snuffing the candlelight. Standing motionless in the sudden darkness, my mind fills with a sense of danger.

I am not alone.

A cold shiver touches my spine. I turn to leave, but the door is lost in the shadows. The cold shiver becomes a tremor of fear. I cannot run. I cannot even move my feet. Barely breathing, I listen and wait.

Beyond the rippled window glass, moonlit snowflakes dance and swirl at the will and mercy of the relentless winter wind.

A man's voice, low and intense, cuts hoarsely through the silence of the night.

"Hurry, girl!"

I blinked several times when I opened my eyes. The room was white, and the light from a large window seemed to shine from every direction.

"Katherine?"

I slowly turned my head and saw Clarisse, wearing jeans and a man's rugby shirt, sitting in the chair by my bed. Her lack of costume, apparently set aside for the day, did not alter the ethereal beauty of her face or the tilt of her blue eyes.

I looked around the room. Unable to make sense of where I was, I turned back toward her.

"Clarisse?"

"Yes?"

"Did I die?"

"No," she said, shaking her head. "You're in a hospital. It was a little touch and go, but you didn't fall very far and, luckily, landed on a pile of rugs the floor finishers had moved into the stairwell. You didn't break anything, but Marcus and I were worried when we couldn't wake you."

"Your story wasn't real, was it?"

She laughed softly. "No. It's just one of several scripts we are rehearsing for when the house opens. Erasmus, you know, left small amounts of money to three young women in his will. I am supposed to be one of them. Tourists like that sort of story re-enactment, you know."

It wasn't real, I repeated to myself. "What's actually in the chamber above that room?"

"There is no chamber above the room we were in. Just attic space. Although history says it was in Basel, no one knows exactly *where* in Basel Erasmus died."

My mind screamed, *But I was there! I was there!* I swallowed and asked, "Did he really die on this date?"

"Um, Katherine, you've been unconscious for three days. But yes, to the best of our knowledge, the day you visited was the anniversary of the day he died. That wasn't part of the original script. I decided to improvise that dialogue because I thought you intentionally chose that date."

"I've been here for three days?" I asked in disbelief.

"Yes, your parents are arriving this afternoon to take you home. They'll be happy to see that you're awake."

The nurse walked into the room, and Clarisse stood to leave. Pausing at the door, she looked back at me. "So, how did I do?"

I smiled at her. "You convinced me."

As she turned, I called her back. "Clarisse! One quick question before you leave. Who knocked on the ceiling? Was it Marcus?"

"What knocks?"

"The two short raps, you know, when you looked up at the end."

"There were no raps this time, but there will be at some point. Marcus is still working on the timing."

"I heard them."

"Probably just random street noises."

I nodded. "Probably."

She waved as she closed the door.

My parents came, gathered my luggage and papers, and took me home. Although I had a headache for several weeks and bruises from falling, there was no lasting damage. I wrote the paper, graduated, and most of this memoir was written from my notes, as much of the experience has faded.

Some memories, however, are unforgettable.

They come to me at night when snow flurries dance at the window, and the scent of lavender drifts on the air. Once again, I am in his chamber, his arms holding my body close, his legs wrapped around mine as his skin slowly absorbs my warmth. With a sigh, I close my eyes at the sound of whispered prayers lost in the smoky fragrance of a small fire.

Finis

Written in memory of Desiderius Erasmus Roterodamus
1466-1536
More: https://plato.stanford.edu/entries/erasmus/

The Bookbinder's Apprentice

"In that book which is my memory,
on the first page of the chapter
that is the day when I first met you,
appear the words, 'Here begins a new life.'"
– Dante Alighieri, *Vita Nuova*

The Bookbinder's Apprentice

No one remembers the bookstore on Old Main Street, or even remembers there ever being a bookstore downtown. "No," they've said to me, "if there had been a bookstore, I would know it!" As though a bookstore—any bookstore—was a siren's call that could not be denied or a beacon whose light would surely reach into their lives by its very existence.

Perhaps the noon sky was too bright, and they did not see a beacon, or maybe they were listening to other voices and did not hear the siren's call on that midsummer's afternoon when a single hour lasted a thousand years.

But I did.

The Bookshop

It was the blue door that caught my attention. Situated at the end of brightly lit window displays and festive "welcome" signs, it appeared older and shabbier than any other door scattered among the downtown shops. Walking over to take a closer look, I noticed the blue paint had worn down in places, revealing a bright green, and beneath that, a brownish-gray patina covered the dark wood.

Chipped gilt lettering, "Books – Old and New," curved above the door. An address, 112B, was freshly stenciled in smudged white paint on the rusting black mailbox hanging loosely on the stucco next to it. I've always been an avid reader, and this shop looked like every bookstore in the small town of my childhood. Although I was on my lunch hour and only had a short time, I felt an irresistible urge to go inside. The tarnished brass knob turned and turned in my hand, but the door didn't open. *Perhaps the store is closed,* I thought. After all, it *was* noon on a Tuesday, and many of the downtown shops were only open two or three days a week during the hot Florida summers.

As I went into my usual sandwich shop for a takeout salad, I wondered why I hadn't noticed the bookstore before, but I was trying to fit more walking into my day and had decided to follow the sidewalk around the edge of downtown instead of taking the more direct route.

I worked for a law firm on the corner of North Palm Street and Apopka Avenue, and, as their only real estate closing paralegal, I had an office to myself. I liked to get takeout because I could close the door and eat my lunch in peace, privacy, and air conditioning. If growing up in Florida had taught me anything, it was the importance of air conditioning.

Deciding to take the same route back to my office, strains of Chris Isaak's "Wicked Game" drifted from a passing car, and I smiled. Humming along, I noticed someone walking out of the bookstore I had seen earlier. I picked up my pace but didn't arrive before the door closed. With a hopeful smile, I approached the store, put my hand on the doorknob, and tried again.

This time, the knob turned easily in my hand, and the door swung open as though, in my brief absence, the lock and hinges had been oiled and polished. Entering the shop, I felt the warmth of daylight streaming in from the skylights above the bookcases where thousands of books were neatly lined up on display. Despite the age of its outside appearance, the inside of the bookstore looked brand-new. The door closed silently behind me, and I was swept into a delightful tangle of fragrances from books, wood smoke, and chocolate.

"Oh, my," I said, looking for a candle or incense burner. I wasn't sure what was causing that wonderful bouquet of scents, but I hoped it was for sale.

"It isn't," said a man's voice to my left.

I immediately turned in the direction of the voice. He stood behind a computer at the sales counter. He was tall, not young, but not old, not handsome, but dignified. His amber-tinted computer glasses disguised the color of his eyes. He was neatly dressed in a blue Oxford shirt and khakis, but no tie. In my thirty-second assessment, the feature I found most remarkable about him was his smile. It was confident, easy, and welcoming.

"What 'isn't'?" I asked.

"The fragrance that is entrancing you, it's not for sale."

"I'm entranced, am I?" I laughed.

"Aren't you?" he said, walking around the counter. "Follow me."

I glanced around quickly and realized I was the only customer in the store.

"No. No, thanks. I think I'll just get back to my office. I only have an hour for lunch. I'll, um, I'll stop back by when I have more time." I turned toward the door.

"Well, you can try, but the owner keeps crazy hours. I'm only here today as a special favor to him. And, speaking of special, I wasn't going far; I just wanted to offer you this."

"What?"

"The source of the sweetness in the air that made you smile when you entered the shop."

He walked to the other side of the room, and I edged around the entryway to see a fully stocked beverage counter. Large and lavish, the bar offered a variety of teas and coffees, assorted cookies, and decadent chocolate biscotti standing upright like spears in a lidded glass canister.

I walked over to look at the display. "This is lovely," I said.

"Thank you." He smiled and added, "The particular aroma you noticed when you walked in is this blend," he said, touching an unmarked tin canister. "I had just brewed some for myself."

"Tea or coffee?"

"Tea."

"And I can't buy it?"

"Ah, no. I'm sorry. We don't have a license to sell food or beverages, so everything you see here is free to our customers, but, regretfully, you were leaving. Perhaps, next time."

He left me standing there as he circled back to the counter on the other side. Without giving me a second thought, he took the top volume from a tall stack of books. Opening it to the first page, he began entering information into the computer. The keystrokes echoed in the stillness of the store. I glanced at the clock above the door; there were still thirty minutes left of my lunch hour.

I stepped back from the beverage bar where he could see me. "Well," I said.

He looked up like he had forgotten I was there. "Yes?"

"I do have time to browse if I eat my lunch very fast when I get back to my office."

He smiled, and I felt myself blushing.

"Then perhaps you would like some refreshment while you browse?"

"Whatever you're having smells divine. I'd like to try that."

"Of course." He returned to where I was standing.

I backed out of his way, and it seemed like only a moment later that he was handing me an insulated cup. "If you're going to browse, it's always better to have a lid," he said. "We have a strict damage policy."

"If I splash it, I have to buy it, right?" I asked teasingly as I took a sip of the tea.

"That's one way of putting it," he said, "but it's always best to be careful. Many of our books, for one reason or another, are difficult to find. And you never know. You may inadvertently damage a book that my next customer has been looking for all her life." He paused, then added, "And it has been my experience that a disappointed customer always leaves empty-handed. We wouldn't want that, would we?"

"No, of course not. I'll be very careful . . . not a single drop! Besides, this tastes exactly as wonderful as it smells, so I would hate to miss one sip."

Actually, I hadn't told him the truth. The tea tasted better than its aroma. My senses fairly danced to the notes of cinnamon, vanilla, anise, and chocolate, combined with a hint of sweet wood smoke that reminded me of lapsang souchong, a black tea roasted over burning wood. It complemented the smell of paper and ink so well that it was hard to separate the taste of the tea from the scent of the books.

I paused as I turned toward the shelves and looked back in his direction. He was once again standing behind the sales counter, entering data into the computer. I glanced at his shirt pocket to ask a question, but noticed he wasn't wearing a name badge.

"Excuse me, I'm sorry to bother you again, but do you have any classic literature written by women authors?"

"Yes, we do. On your right, against the wall."

I looked at him without moving.

"Is there anything else?" he asked.

"No. Well, yes. In the event I have another question, may I ask your name?"

"Of course. If you need anything, you can call me Aidan."

"I can 'call' you Aidan? Isn't it your name?"

"No, but it's the one I use when I work here. You can blame my father for giving me a name that is very difficult to pronounce."

"Okay. In that case, nice to meet you, Aidan. You make a great cup of tea. You may call me Helena."

"That's not your real name, is it?"

"No, but it's what you can call me when I shop here."

He smiled in response to my sassiness. "Very well . . . Helena. I hope you find something that pleases you. I'll be right here if you have any other questions."

I lifted my cup in acknowledgment and turned back to the bookcases. My lunch hour was rapidly dwindling, and I wanted to find something I liked, if for no other reason, so I would have a reason to talk to him again.

I walked up and down the short aisles and past rows of shelves. Although there were a lot of books, I was surprised that the fiction selection was so limited. Some of the books, as promised by the gilded sign above the door, were new, but most were older titles. Examining the books in the section he'd pointed out to me, I was disappointed to see that there wasn't anything I hadn't already read half a dozen times. I followed the rows up and down, checking titles and authors' names, but found nothing I wanted to read.

Reaching the end of the last row, I noticed an unlatched door. Glancing through the narrow shaft of rainbow-tinted light, I saw beautifully bound books gleaming on polished shelves. Thinking it was a rare book room, I walked over for a closer look. The "DO NOT ENTER" sign on the wall next to the door and an identical sign on the door paled in significance to the sight of the most resplendent books I had ever seen. I opened the door a little wider and stepped inside.

These books were not stacked on one another or set upon their spines and squeezed together in bookcases. They were displayed on angled revolving shelves that rotated up and down at a touch. The books were alphabetized by author and perfectly spaced so they could lie open without overlapping the book next to them. Exquisitely bound in dark red leather, the titles gleamed with elegant gold lettering. When I carefully lifted the cover of the one nearest to me, I found the words were also printed in gold ink. With their gold-tipped pages, they looked more like collector's items than real books. I checked the cover and saw that the one I had opened was *Little Women* by Louisa May Alcott. It was the most precious edition I had ever seen. I lifted the volume from the shelf. It felt warm and fit snugly in my hand as if it were made especially for me.

I thought I heard someone talking behind me, but I was so fascinated by the book I was holding that I didn't turn around. I tried to juggle my purse, deli bag, and tea so I could get a closer look, but I was holding too many things. Forgetting for a moment that the shelf was slanted, I set my cup where the book had been. At that moment, my purse slipped from my shoulder and bumped into the shelf. As though in slow motion, I watched in horror as the shelf began to rotate and the cup containing my tea tilted toward me. I caught it before it spilled onto the shelf, but not before it splashed a few drops on the book I held in my other hand.

Less than a moment later, the book was taken from me as I fished for a napkin in my deli bag.

"What have you done?" Aidan's voice had gone up an entire octave, and his eyes flashed from the book in his hand to my face.

"I'm sorry. I accidentally splashed a little tea on the cover. It's leather, so I'm sure it will clean up okay."

"It will not 'clean up okay.' I called your name several times to tell you that the books back here are not for sale, but you kept walking. I even raised my voice as I was running to stop you, and still, you did not look around."

He looked at me sternly. "Perhaps if you had told me your real name, you would have paid better attention to what I was saying."

Then he cradled the book as though I had ruined his most cherished possession.

"We must take this to the back right away to see if it can be salvaged." He walked to the front door and locked it. Returning to the book room, he took me by the hand.

"I can't be in two places at once," he said, leading the way.

Feeling too guilty to argue, I reluctantly followed him past the gleaming books. I wanted to reach out my hand toward their gold-embossed leather covers, but after my little mishap, I was too scared to touch them. I looked back at the clock above the front door; it read twelve forty-five. I hoped the book wouldn't take long to clean.

Aidan held back a curtain of crystal beads threaded on golden strands that separated the two rooms so I could pass through them, and then followed. I thought the beaded walkway was an unexpected bohemian touch and watched as the sparkling threads swayed and fell back into place.

As I turned around to follow Aidan, I stopped. I had not entered a store manager's office or even a stockroom. Opening before me was a large, curved room resembling a sphere cut in half. The only flat part of the space was the floor; the walls were high and curved, creating a domed ceiling of light. Momentarily dazed, I looked back to orient myself with the front of the store, but I could no longer see it or the golden strands we had just walked through.

I shook my head; it had to be an optical illusion. It was impossible that this space was part of the one-story shops lining the red brick streets of a hot and dusty downtown in central Florida.

The Bookseller

"Where in the heck am I?" I whispered to myself.

I looked at Aidan and said as earnestly as I could, "Listen, I'm real sorry about the book. Truly, I am, but I have exactly fifteen minutes to get back to work. Just tell me how much it will cost to repair the damage—or even replace the book—and I'll pay you. I know it is a really nice edition and probably very expensive, but I'll get the money to you somehow."

He calmly removed his glasses. "I really dislike wearing these," he said, slipping them into his shirt pocket, "but I dislike the computer glare more." Then he looked at me, and I found myself falling into the rain-swept depths of his eyes.

"First questions are answered first," he said as I stared wordlessly at his face. "Where are you? You are in a fourth-dimensional time slip. You may—or may not—know that Einstein once proposed that the fourth dimension was time itself, so without boring you with all the physics of our exact location, I can say that we have slipped into a place where time exists only as a concept, not a reality."

I blinked to break my stare. "I'm sorry, what? What are you talking about?"

"I'm talking about a time slip," he continued calmly. "For instance, consider air in your three-dimensional world. It exists but surrounds you invisibly and, therefore, does not define your existence within your world. Here, in this bubble of sorts, there is no 'fifteen minutes' to get back to work. No twenty-four-hour day, Tuesday does not exist, and neither does this week, month, or year. Yet, time is all around us, a vast, immeasurable progression of existence."

Who talked like this? When did time ever not exist? "You cannot possibly be serious," I said.

"I am absolutely serious; there is no 'time' here."

"Like Heaven?" I blurted out.

"What do you know about Heaven?"

"Just what I learned while growing up in the Baptist church, that is, until I married an Episcopalian."

He smiled and shook his head. "Not the frame of reference I'd pick for accuracy. So, the answer to your question is 'No. Not like Heaven.' To understand Heaven, you must remove the word 'progression' from my previous definition. In Heaven, you stay as you are; a timeless existence as a static soul. Joyous, loving, and beautiful, yes, but with no individual inner fire or ambition to compete with the divine spark of the shared consciousness of God."

"Because you become a better person in Heaven?"

"No, because of the lack of desire, means, and opportunity to do evil. It is Heaven. If you didn't belong there, you would not have ascended there."

Although our conversation had leapt beyond the bounds of incredulity, my confusion was changing to curiosity. Finding his detailed descriptions fascinating, I decided to play along and asked, "How do you know this? Are you an angel?"

Aidan turned around for a moment, then faced me again. "Did you see any wings on me?"

"Um, no." I thought for a moment. "No progression."

"No physical progression; my body is the same as it has always been."

"But why are you here? Were love, joy, and infinite days of glory not enough? Was being part of the shared consciousness of the divine spark not enough?" I asked.

"Yes, they were, for a very long time, but in the last millennia or two, spirits began arriving with stories of the proliferation of literature, music, art, and poetry, and then they spoke of inventions that not only allowed people to fly, but permitted them to travel beyond the boundaries of Earth and live to tell about it, and other machines that could capture voices in the air, preserve, and replay them. All those memories, sights, and sounds that I could never share—and much that I would never understand—because my intellect, like my soul, was already perfect and could not expand."

He smiled slightly and shook his head. "You cannot 'sin' in Heaven, you know, but if you could, the only sin would be unhappiness. It's almost a contradiction in terms, as in, 'if you were unhappy, then you surely could not be in Heaven,' for what more could one soul ask?"

"Indeed . . . , but you asked?"

"Yes."

"And?"

"Look around you. It is quite obvious that I am no longer in Heaven. I'm just a spirit who let his curiosity get the better of him, so I am here. Satisfying my curiosity for knowledge and experiences while making books for transport."

Suddenly, I had an image of him gathering up the books and flying away with them, and I almost smiled at the thought. Intrigued, I wanted to know more, and, managing to keep a straight face, I asked, "Where are they going?"

"Each book you saw with a red cover has been transported to a library in Heaven. That is why they must remain undamaged, for perfection is the only standard Heaven allows. What you've seen is less a bookstore than a book safe, so whenever anything happens to one of *my* books, it must be remade, and that is why you, my dear whatever-your-real-name-is, are here in this room."

"To repair the damage to the book? I'm sure all I need is some dust spray and a paper towel."

"Ah, no. That would leave smudges and infinitesimal scratches. You must remake the book."

"You must remake the book," echoed in my mind, driving away all thoughts of humor. I took a step back. I could not have

heard him correctly. How could I remake a book? It was impossible. Of all the things he had said since coming through the crystal curtain that could not possibly be real, this was his most outlandish comment of them all—and the scariest because I could see he meant every word.

"Wait, just a minute. Are you kidnapping me?" I sputtered.

***

Aidan turned his full attention on her—something he had avoided until that moment.

Like many of the women who wandered into his shop, she was not quite refined, not quite pretty, and not quite smart enough to warrant his consideration. It was as though she had stopped just short of perfection somewhere in her life and decided there was no reason to go any further. He tried to keep the look of annoyance from his face. It had become increasingly difficult to find someone who could amuse him anymore, and there was not much time left to attract a customer far more accomplished than the woman standing in front of him. However, despite what either of them wanted, the book was more important.

"Interesting concept," he said, "but let's examine the facts. You're not a 'kid,' and you knew there would be consequences if you damaged any of the books, which," he pointed accusingly at the book in his hand, "you clearly did. Therefore, the answer is, 'No, I'm not kidnapping you.' I have merely brought you into a space to give you the opportunity to repair the damage you caused—not just to the book itself, but to the collection of books that *I* created that were never meant for you. It is my expectation that you will show your gratitude to resolve this act of deliberate negligence by doing the very best work of which you are capable."

She was silent for a moment, then, taking a deep breath, nodded. "Okay," she said, "everything you've said is true, and I am sorry. I do want to make this right, but, Aidan, what you're expecting me to do is impossible."

Spreading his arms wide to encompass the entirety of the room, he said, "Nothing is impossible while you are here."

The Scriptorium

But where was "here"?

I looked from him to the space around us. I could see that it was a workroom of sorts, with stacks of paper, rolls of red leather standing in a barrel, and on a large desk, a cloth concealing some kind of machinery. There were two smaller desks with chairs and a huge wooden chest with drawers about an inch and a half high. Shelves filled with hundreds, if not thousands, of books—tall, short, and colorfully bound—curved to the left until I could no longer see them. There was nothing else in the room except three doors on the right side, none of which were marked "Exit." It was impossible to believe that, even in my dreams, I could ever imagine such a room. I tried to fight down creeping feelings of dread.

"Aidan, am I still alive?"

"Of course. Why would you think otherwise? If you were dead, you would be of little use to me."

I thought about that, then asked, "If you're a spirit, then why would I be of little use as a spirit?"

"Because your spirit would have moved on to Heaven or Hell. It would not stay here."

"You are a spirit, and you are here."

"Yes. This is my space," he said, with an air of exasperation. "It may not seem like much to you, but it's all I want. I suspect you want streets of gold, white robes, and halos. You will not find those items here."

"I'm sorry about all the questions. I'm just trying to understand. Just to clear up one more thing, if this isn't Heaven, are we in Hell?"

He looked at me calmly. "If we were in Hell, you would not have to ask that question."

"I see. Well, that's good to know." I laughed nervously as I glanced around the space, looking for something—anything—familiar. "Who would have ever thought that the fourth dimension is a big round room behind a bookstore?"

"No one. Which is why it is perfect for my work. And it isn't a big round room. Have you ever seen the inside of a nautilus shell? An inner spiral with chambers on either side?"

"I've seen pictures."

"This space is constructed much like that, with a curving central corridor with rooms that are arranged as I require them. Entire areas, including those for access to the Earth dimension, are constantly evolving. For example, it hasn't always been a bookstore. When I first became interested in bookmaking, I created this workspace as a scriptorium attached to a 6th-century Benedictine monastery. I hid the portal behind a tapestry and borrowed their books at night, returning them by morning."

"I'm not sure I know what a scriptorium is."

"It's a Latin word that translates into English as 'writing room' and was once used to describe the chambers where monks and their scribes copied, illustrated, and bound books. That is what I do here."

"Well, that's certainly what it looks like. But, wait a minute! You were serious? Do you really expect me to remake the whole book before I leave?"

"Why, yes. If you had only damaged the cover, you would have only had to replace the cover, but see, a few drops of the tea spilled over onto the pages, and they are already discolored and becoming wavy. This is not acceptable, so it must be entirely remade."

"But I have to get back to work!" I glanced at my watch. The second hand had stopped moving. I shook my wrist, but it would not restart. I took out my phone. The screen was black. I looked up at Aidan. "There's no service back here."

"No, not now, not ever. Mechanical devices do not work in this space; there is no electricity, and while I have the materials to build a small steam engine, why would I?"

"But there is light."

"Ah, yes, there is always light. It washes over my small piece of the universe like a desert breeze brushes over the sand."

"Is that a quotation from some book you've read—or made?"

"No, it is the truth of the light."

"Well, that sounds very poetic and all, but you don't understand. I must get back to work. Perhaps I can return this evening and get started on the book. I don't mind; my evenings are usually free, but I'm going to be late, and people will worry if I'm not there."

"You *will* go back to work—if that is so important to you—when the book is remade. Also, for your information, they will never know you were gone."

"So, the world is just going to go on without me. I have coworkers and friends. Eventually, someone will notice."

"No, the world you left is not 'going to go on' at all, and no one will notice."

I opened my mouth to speak, but I could not form a coherent thought.

"Yes, I see you're confused." He took my hand and guided me to a chair. "We'll start from the beginning. Well," he laughed to himself, "maybe not *the* beginning. We'll start from five minutes ago when you entered the time slip. In other words, you slipped out at a certain point in time in the Earth world, and when you have finished your task, you will slip back in that same moment. It's all very simple."

"But—"

"Nothing in your body will change. All molecular advancement was suspended when you walked through the portal. The factors that would age you do not exist here. You will not be any more tired than you are now; you will not be hungry or thirsty. I promise you, everything you were when you walked through the front door will still be precisely the same when you walk out of it."

"You mean like the woman who walked out just before me. Was she in a . . . in a time slip?"

He smiled and shook his head. "No. She walked in and asked if I had any books by local authors. I told her that, regrettably, I did not, so she left."

"Didn't stay long enough to have tea?"

"No. She chose not to be a customer."

Suddenly wishing I had been so lucky, I tried again. "Couldn't we take this book apart and see if replacing the damaged pages is enough? Seems like a waste to throw it all away."

"There are two problems with your suggestion, Helena. One is that no two printers compose exactly the same. As you replace the damaged pages, it may seem *to you* that they are identical to the work I've done, but you would be wrong. Even minuscule variations can affect the continuity of the transference of the book, thereby interfering with the reader's understanding. Secondly, you say 'take this book apart' as though that process will not damage even more pages, the spine, and possibly the entire inner structure of the book, thereby making it impossible to reassemble. So, no, I'm quite sure the book will need to be completely remade and remade by one person. As I have other tasks for which I am responsible, this book is yours."

"But, Aidan, I have no experience in composing or printing or anything like that! I think you are being overly optimistic."

"Perhaps, but you are here, and I am here to help, so it will be done. It's quite new to me, too. I've never actually had an apprentice."

"Is that what I am?"

"Well, it sounds better than vandal."

"I hardly think that is true. I didn't *mean* to damage the book."

"Did you *mean* to walk into a room that had a sign—a large sign—that clearly said, 'Do not enter' on the wall *and* on the door?"

"Yes. Yes, I did."

He didn't say another word; he just looked at me for a few moments. Then he glanced down at the stain on the back cover and touched the dampness on top of the pages. Sighing once again as if he had lost something dear to him, he set the book carefully on the table.

"Let's get started," he said, motioning me to join him.

I stood and walked toward the worktable, still laden down with my purse, the half-emptied cup of tea, and my lunch. He regarded me critically. Then shook his head.

"That won't do," he said. "You need to put those things away and take off your clothes."

"What?!" I stopped moving. "I am not going to do that."

He tilted his head and looked at me. "Why not?" His expression of surprise was soon followed by one of acknowledgment, and he began to laugh. "Oh, no, you don't understand."

"I understand perfectly when a man who has me alone in a room tells me to take off my clothes!" I turned and began walking in the other direction. "I'm sure there's a way out of here somewhere."

"Helena, please stop." His voice was gentle, and there was no laughter in his words. "You misunderstood what I meant. Although your body won't change while you are in this dimension, your clothes will age, discolor, and perhaps become stained with the work you're going to do; even your scuffed shoes will become more worn, and I have no way of replacing them.

There is nothing in your purse that you will need, and you won't get hungry. To ensure your belongings stay in their current condition, they must be put away. I will dispose of your cup to prevent further accidents and then bring you a container to safeguard your things so they will not deteriorate. Even though I am not sure how long it will take to replace the book, I promised to deliver you back to the world in the same condition I found you, and so I shall."

"What do you expect me to wear while I'm in here?"

"What I wear, of course. A smock or lab coat with short sleeves."

I sat in the nearest chair. "I'll wait," I said.

About ten minutes later, he returned with a small chest, a four-panel screen, and some white cloth thrown over his arm. Without moving to help him, I watched as he set up the screen in front of the rows of books in the left hallway. He set the small box behind it and turned toward where I was sitting.

"This should fit you," he said, handing me a white garment that looked like a smock made from a man's white dress shirt. Roomy and shapeless, I didn't know whether to be grateful or insulted. He was wearing one like a lab coat over his clothes.

"I can wear it over my clothes; it's big enough," I said.

"No, I've already explained to you why you cannot. No one is waiting beyond the shop door for me, and even if someone were, I have other clothes. Regretfully, you do not, so we must protect the ones you have." He pointed to the screen. "You can change there," he said. "Just put your things in the box. I'll store it later."

I looked at the screen and back at him. "Just don't forget where you put it."

"Can't forget . . . anything," he said slowly.

I walked behind the screen.

"Aidan?"

"I'm over here by the desk, Helena. And, before you ask, you are outside my line of sight."

I couldn't see him, so maybe he was, and maybe he wasn't. I did not know him well enough to trust him, so I quickly slid the smock over my head. It fell around me in folds like a tent, and using it like one, I removed my clothes beneath the cover of the soft white cotton fabric.

Unsure of how long I would be there, it made sense to put my things away. Opening the wooden box, I noticed that it was lined with gray metal and just large enough for everything to fit inside perfectly. I thought about the deli salad, but I didn't have any appetite for even a taste, so I packed it away with everything else. There was even room for my *slightly* scuffed shoes.

I looked down at the shirt I was now wearing; there was certainly nothing provocative about it. Long enough to be a dress, I found myself wishing I had a belt. I thought about taking my shoes out of the box when I discovered a pair of socks tucked into one of the shirt pockets. They were too big for me, but running around barefoot was something I rarely did, even at home. When I pulled them up, the tops almost reached my knees.

Feeling more like a dork than an apprentice, I walked toward the worktable. I swear I saw him smother a smile.

I sat down in the chair across from him. "Okay," I said, "here I am, all dressed up in my apprentice clothes. Now that I've settled in, more or less, let's pretend I don't know anything about science, and please explain to me again where I am."

"I don't think any 'pretending' will be involved," he said. "All right, for what I sincerely hope is the last time, I will go through it once again. The bookstore you entered exists in the third dimension—we'll call it the Earth dimension or Earth world. When we came through the portal, we entered a fourth-dimensional space. To make things simpler, we will use your word. We'll call it the 'divine' dimension."

"So, I *am* in Heaven."

"No, not in the way you think of Heaven, perhaps. However, a 16th-century scholar named Erasmus once said, 'Your library is your Paradise.' If we use that definition, then you *are* in my version of Heaven."

"How long will I stay in your Paradise?"

"As long as it takes to make a book."

"You live here?"

"Why, yes. Though 'living' is a very third-dimensional concept."

"Are you dead?"

"Do I look dead to you?"

"No."

"I am a spirit; this is a physical manifestation of my body that allows me to do the kind of work I want to do."

"Are you saying you're immortal?"

"Only inasmuch as you are—a body of flesh that will, at some point, self-destruct and decay, with an immortal spirit—exactly like you."

"Not exactly like me."

"No? Like you, my mortal body is flesh. My immortal spirit, again like yours, belongs to God, the Creator, with justice and mercy."

Too embarrassed to admit I still didn't understand, I said, "Well, Aidan, I admit it's not the craziest thing I've ever heard, but it's close. You sound as though you may have been a philosopher at one time."

"I have been many things, but regardless of what I once was, I am now a printer and a bookbinder. The only philosophy I know is what I've read; the conjectures and beliefs, however, are my own, as I am sure yours belong to you."

"But if you have no life beyond this space, what is the difference between this and death?"

He smiled. "I get to make books."

"How long do you have to do this?"

"I don't *have* to do it at all. It's my choice." He looked around and smiled. "This *is* my Paradise, Helena. For as long as I am happy here, I'm allowed to be here."

"Are you happy here?"

"Yes. I learn, my mind grows, and I discover new ideas every day."

"But you're alone."

"Not now," he said. "Shall we begin?"

"We're really doing this?"

"Yes. You've promised to stay until my book is replaced, so we may as well get started."

"Um, okay. By the way, just how long does it take to make a book?

"Because I don't stop once I've begun, I can usually create a book in three weeks, Earth time, but since I'm teaching you, it may take longer. Then again, since I will be helping you, it may even out. We will see if two heads and four hands are better than mine alone."

"You mean you've never done this before? I can't be the only person who has accidentally damaged a book in the entire history of—. What is the name of this bookshop anyway?"

"When the bookshop first opened in Amsterdam in the mid-1600s, it was called the Dutch equivalent of 'Leaves of Change,' but I have always preferred 'Books Old and New' as it is more accurate. The tree is just a residual image of what it once represented. The owner likes it, so we've kept it. And yes, others have, in one way or another, damaged the books in the front part of the store. I let them pay for the damaged book, and they can either take it or discard it, as they wish. You, however, are the only one who has ever damaged one of *my* books. My fault," he confessed, "for not making sure the door was locked."

"Or closed."

"The door was not open."

"Well, a little open. Ajar, actually."

"And the sign on the door that said, 'Do not enter'?"

"I was too mesmerized by the rainbow light to see it until I reached the doorway, and then, well, I saw all those beautiful books, and it was too late. It was impossible for me to leave without going in that room."

"And now you are in this room. You would be yawning your way through your afternoon assignments by now if you hadn't been so clumsy—or momentarily blind."

"Or if you had locked the door."

"Yes."

"Aidan, may I ask a question before we start the process of my learning to make books?"

"Another one?"

"Yes. What would have happened if I had accidentally spilled tea on one of the books in the front of the store?"

"Since all the books in that section of the shop are the same price, I would have charged you twelve dollars for the book you damaged and banned you from the store."

"Banned me from the store? For how long?"

"Why, forever, of course."

"That seems harsh."

"Such carelessness cannot be risked twice."

"Or forgiven?"

He did not answer right away but glanced down at the book on the table.

"We are lucky that we have the original book as a template, or you would have to set the type and hope it fits within the page margins and that it ends cleanly without leaving sentence bits at the bottom or leftover at the top of the next page. We also know which typeface and font to use and the spacing. Fitting and refitting the spacing of the type can be tedious because it all must be perfectly matched throughout the book. By not having to start from, um, scratch, I believe it's called, there will be less room for errors, and we will avoid the waste of reprinting."

"Printing? Do you expect me to print the entire book? By *hand*?"

"Of course not. Your handwriting is probably untrained, inconsistent, and uneven." He removed the cover from the piece of machinery sitting on the table. It was smaller than any I'd ever seen and spotlessly clean, but despite its mechanical simplicity, I recognized it at once. It was a letterpress. A one-page-at-a-time printing press.

"How skilled are you at reading English backward? Oh, well, it doesn't matter; you'll catch on quickly enough. Luckily, though, we don't have to depend on your grammar skills or your ability to spell; the words, letters, and spaces are right in front of you, so there should be no mistakes."

***

He opened another drawer and took out a stack of paper that was at least twice as wide as the book.

"Why is the paper so wide?" I asked.

"Because we print two pages per sheet and fold them in half in sections of twelve sheets. But we only use the right half of each side of the paper; we do not print double-sided. Most of the pages will be out of order when you print them because they are folded inside each other, but you are lucky; all the planning work for which pages to print on every single sheet has already been done for you . . . by me."

"Sure, I understand."

"Do you? Do you also understand that even if the first half is printed perfectly and you make an error in the printing of the second half, it will be necessary for you to reprint both halves again and again until both pages are perfect?"

I looked from the book to the stack of paper. "Oh, my," I whispered to myself.

"Yes. Perhaps, by now, you are beginning to comprehend why the destruction of any of these books is so hurtful to me."

"Yes, I can see that," I said, reaching my hand out to touch his wrist. "Aidan, I am sorry I was so careless."

"That is easy to say now. Tell me how sorry you are after you have ruined a dozen sheets of paper because your spacing is off, and you must reprint a page for the thirteenth time . . . or the thirtieth. Perhaps then you will sound as though you actually mean it."

He pulled his hand away and turned to leave the room.

"Where are you going?"

"We're going to need more paper.

***

To prepare for my new position as apprentice printer, I took advantage of his absence to take a closer look at the press and do a quick inventory of the tools and supplies on the table. The work area itself was a combination of an apothecary cabinet and a workbench. Dozens of wooden drawers of different sizes were set into the curve of the wall above the work surface, and beneath them were two shelves holding various items ranging from large wooden clamps to long, delicate needles and spools of thread. My scrutiny stopped abruptly as I contemplated why needles and thread were necessary to make a book.

I looked up when Aidan set the stack of paper on the worktable.

"Where do we start?"

"Where every book starts, with a good story to tell. Which of my books did you destroy?"

I thought that particularly callous, but I suppose I had "destroyed" it in his eyes. I turned the book over on the table and pointed to the front cover.

"*Little Women* by Louisa May Alcott."

"Yes," he said, reciting from memory, "American author, published in the United States, 1869. Genre: coming-of-age. Category: Historical/American Civil War Fiction, cross-referenced Women's Literature, cross-referenced Biographical and/or Semi-Biographical. Considered an American Classic but not literary canon. Very popular with female readers of all ages." Then he smiled and looked at me. "How old were you the first time you read it?"

"Eight or nine," I confessed. "I was one of those little girls who read under the covers at night with a flashlight. I think I read this book in three days. I loved it."

"And how many times since then?"

"I'm not sure . . . probably five or six."

"No wonder you picked it up; it was like home to you."

I looked at him. How amazingly astute he could be, yet sometimes seemed so clueless. "Yes, that is exactly why I picked it up."

"But you did not pick up the used copy on the shelves near the wall."

"No."

"Strictly from a bookseller's point of view, why this one and not that one?"

"This one is so beautiful. It's like the book reflects my love for the story just by existing."

"Well said. Now you know why it must be remade. Perfectly. Exactly as it is here."

"As you wish," I said.

"The Princess Bride!" he said, smiling.

"Perhaps," I said. Still baffled by the workroom, the printing press, and my . . . my host? Mentor? Tutor? Colleague? Boss? I shook my head as though I were dreaming and thought, *Inconceivable.*

Wanting to get this show on the road so I could get back to my life, I asked, "What do we do after we find a story worth telling?"

"We compose."

"Compose? Like creative writing?"

"No. As you can see, the narrative is already quite wonderfully written. You must set the type to print each page." He lifted the cover and looked at the first page. "Wait here while I get the appropriate type drawer for the title page."

"Okay."

He pulled an entire drawer out of the chest and brought it over to the table. I stared at all the small compartments containing silver letters and punctuation marks, hundreds, maybe thousands, of them.

"Aidan, why can't we do this on your computer? I'm really good at that. I've even composed and printed a small directory using a publishing program. It turned out nice, and I liked doing it, too. It would be so much easier."

He stared down at the type drawer silently for several moments before looking up. "Helena, I told you there is no electricity here."

"But the light?"

"I am not responsible for the light."

"Oh."

"But more than that, *I* create these books from paper and ink that I make from the resources available to me. I want to touch each element and watch the book grow under my hands, not in a plastic box as ones and zeros. And then, when it is finished, I want to hold it—whole, complete, and perfect—and rejoice in my accomplishment. To do this work, to feel that exultation, can you think of one reason why I would surrender any of that pleasure for the sake of mere convenience?"

Although he did not speak loudly or forcefully, I sensed a power beneath his voice that made my words stick in my throat and come out as a whisper, "No, no, I can't."

"No," he said, smiling kindly, "there isn't one." Without waiting for my response, he continued, "Shall we move on?"

I nodded.

He handed me a small but heavy steel tray. "This is called a galley. It is where we compose the page," he said. "There are different ways of doing this, but I prefer to compose the entire page at one time so I know exactly what it will look like when printed. Some compositors use smaller composing sticks, with only a line or paragraph of type at a time. I prefer this method, so this is what we will use."

I looked down at the roughly six-by-nine-inch metal tray in my hands and then back at him. Finally recovering my voice, I said, "Now what?"

"Now we use the damaged book as a pattern. Look at the way the title page is composed and then add the lines of type to the galley to recreate it."

I looked down at the book. Centered on both the line and the page, it read:

Little Women:
or Meg, Jo, Beth, and Amy
Louisa May Alcott
1868-1869
United States – English

"Um, okay. Quick question. If I am composing the entire page, how do I get these large blocks of blank space?"

"With these," he said, indicating blank strips of varying heights and lengths made to fit the width of the composing tray.

"Do you have a ruler?"

"I have a typesetter's ruler," he said, handing me a metal eighteen-inch ruler with descending squares like small windows down its length. "You may have heard it referred to as a pica ruler. It's used for measuring and laying out the type."

"I've never seen or heard of one, regardless of what you call it, but, looking at it, I can see that it would be very useful. Do you have one that is, perhaps, not quite as long?"

"It's the only kind of ruler I have. Perhaps you could try using your eyes to gauge the white space."

"No, I don't want to have to do it twice because I was off a quarter of an inch."

"True, and I admire your optimism. I fully expect it to take you no fewer than twelve attempts before you go on to the first chapter."

I wanted to say something in my defense, but couldn't think of anything and just glared at him in silence.

"Oh, and remember, the type is set backward, right to left. Let me know when you have the galley composed, and then we will move on to step two."

"What is step two?"

"Printing the practice page. It's actually exciting—at least to me—to see how beautifully the gold print lays on the paper."

"Is that real gold?"

"Of course. I'm not even sure how you would go about making fake gold or why you would consider using it."

"Expense, perhaps?"

"Usually not a consideration because it is a naturally occurring metal in both the third and fourth dimensions. Besides, regardless of the cost, nothing else would be as efficient. There is a reason why I have chosen to print my books with gold."

"Well, you just said it is beautiful on the page."

"Yes, but gold is one of the most conductive and least corrosive metallic elements. These books are created to last centuries, so they must be resilient. But, as I was saying, once you have the letters and spacers in perfect order, you then use a paintbrush to paint a line of gold on the pressing glass to match the line of print. Don't hurry. The gold is very slow drying and won't dry completely until it is pressed onto the paper. The application is somewhat of a learning process; too much, and the letter is a blob; too little, and it is incomplete. In fact, you may want to work a practice sheet or two or ten before trying to use gold to print an entire page."

"But what happens to the gold on the practice pages? Surely it isn't tossed away?"

"Nothing is 'tossed away' here. You will scrape the gold from the imperfect or practice pages for reuse with this instrument," he said, picking up a small, curved knife.

"Do I reuse the paper as well?"

"Use paper that has been printed *and* scraped? For *my* books? No. The paper is ruined for future consideration—even for practice, unless you become very, very good at scraping. Any paper that is deemed unusable for practice is shredded to create new paper." He paused for a moment, then added, "See that door?"

I looked at the first of the three doors set into the wall where it curved to the right. "Yes."

"Never go in there."

"Why?"

"I do not need to give you a reason. Have you forgotten what happened the last time you walked into a room that said, 'Do not enter'? Are you willing to risk what may happen a second time?"

Already feeling like Alice deep in the rabbit hole, I didn't want to run into any more dimensions. "No, Aidan, I do not."

"Thank you."

I eyed the door with suspicion but decided it was his house, more or less, not mine. After all, he could be keeping a pet dragon in there—or worse. And whatever "worse" was, I didn't want to know.

I smiled at him and pointed to the book. "Is that all you make with the gold?"

"What else would I make with it?"

"I'm not sure . . . earrings?"

For the first time since I'd walked into the store, I heard Aidan laugh. It sounded like a chorus of voices echoing all at once. Beautiful and irresistible, I couldn't help but laugh in response.

"Oh, Helena, thank you for that! It has been too long since I laughed. And I promise you, in gratitude, when you are finished, I will give you a present—but don't count on earrings."

"Don't worry, I won't."

Printing

As I learned to assemble type while reading right to left, Aidan rearranged the desks within the workspace. First, he folded and moved the screen to the farthest edge of the workroom and tilted it against the wall. Then, he dismantled one of the smaller desks, carried the pieces next to the screen, and began reassembling it. When he had put it back together, he set the screen up between the worktable where I sat and the desk. He came back for the chair.

"Why did you move the desk behind the screen?"

"I have work to do, and I did not wish to disturb your concentration. Sometimes, the least distraction can cause a typesetter to misspell a word or overlook a point of punctuation. This way, I am affording us both a level of privacy to do our own work. Hopefully, that will enable you to make fewer errors."

"I'm not sure what kind of distraction you mean, Aidan, because look what I've done while you were moving things around. I've already finished the title page."

He glanced skeptically at the composing slate. "And you think you've finished?"

"Yes, I've measured, compared, and measured again."

"Hmm, measured twice?"

"Yes. My dad always said, 'Measure twice, cut once.'"

"All right, we'll find out," he said, reaching for a piece of paper and a gray, square rock. Then, opening one of the dozen or so small drawers above the table, he removed the tiniest paintbrush I'd ever seen, a paintbrush about a quarter-inch wide, and a small vial with bright brownish-red liquid.

"If you pay attention to how I do this, I won't have to show you again."

"Of course, I'll watch every move you make."

He took the composing slate and lightly ran the gray rock over the typeface, barely touching the tops of the letters. "This printing is only for placement—not reading—try not to get any dust into the crevices of the closed letters. For efficiency, note that the softer you rub the graphite over the type," he said, "the easier the clean-up."

Although he could not see me, I nodded.

He fitted the galley into the slot at the bottom of the press, placed a piece of paper over the slate, turned the press until it stopped, and then reversed the turn to lift it off the paper. He smiled when he removed the paper. "Here is your first practice page," he said, handing it to me.

"I thought it was going to be in gold," I said, unable to disguise my disappointment at the sight of the light gray print.

"How many times do you want to scrape gold from ruined pages?"

"As few times as possible."

"Then we agree. We won't attempt the gold printing until you have the practice page correct."

I looked down at the sheet of paper in my hand and then back at the original. I'd like to say that it was close, but it was a disaster. The only thing I'd gotten right was the left margin. I tried to smile. "It's a start," I said.

He barely glanced at the page I was holding and nodded. "And yet you measured it . . . twice." He opened another drawer and withdrew a square of white cotton and a small brush. "Use these to clean any residual graphite from the type," he said, "and start over. Also, use them lightly. I don't want to have to teach you how to carve type elements while you're here."

He turned and began walking down the hall.

"Where are you going?"

"To find you a smaller ruler," he said.

I had just finished cleaning the type when he returned with four pieces of another typesetter's ruler cut into different lengths and a small white ball.

"Thank you," I said when he set the ruler pieces on the table. "I'm sure that will make all the difference."

"I'm sure it will," he said, suppressing a smile.

"What's this for?" I asked, lifting the small ball and squishing it between my fingers.

"It's an adhesive putty used to lift the graphite from the paper. Do not rub the paper; just press lightly and lift each mark one at a time. Fold the putty as it gets dirty. Try not to smudge the paper as you move from one line to the next. If you get it clean enough, we may be able to use it for a practice sheet one or two times more."

Having the smaller rulers helped, and he finally approved the sixteenth practice page.

He took out a pane of glass and placed it over the practice page. "See?" he asked, pointing to the letters. "You can read what you've printed through the glass."

I nodded.

"Take this brush and paint the gold ink over all the words you see through the glass. You must use a thin, steady layer without deviation. No blobs, no wavy lines, no weak spots. Questions?"

"Yes, can you show me first?"

"If you think it will help. I explained it quite thoroughly."

"You explained it very well, but I think it will help immensely to watch you do it once. Please, Aidan."

Taking the brush with the quarter-inch wide bristles, he dipped it into the bottle and, within seconds, had painted a straight line on the glass, precisely covering the first line of type. He handed me the brush and walked away.

I had some experience in painting, but nothing like this. The liquid gold was thin and wanted to drip before I could get it to the glass. Then, my lines were not straight enough, and I had to use the ruler to steady my hand. And I knew, even before he held it to the light to see if the paint was evenly distributed on the lines, that there were some thin areas.

He handed me another piece of glass. "Try again," he said. "But before you do, press a clean sheet of paper on the glass so the gold will transfer to the paper. Afterward, you can scrape it off into the bowl. Make sure you get all of it." He turned to leave and then circled back. Reaching into the open drawer, he put two more pieces of glass onto the table. "Just in case," he said. "As I mentioned, the gold dries very slowly on the glass, which is perfect for printing but not for mistakes."

"Thank you," I said reluctantly.

He stopped and looked at me. "Did you think you would get this right without practice? Printing is not a talent that comes naturally. Printing is a skill that must be learned. Some parts of the process may come more easily than others, but no one is born a printer. It takes patience, practice, and a trained eye to excel. Pay attention, take your time, and you'll improve."

"Okay, Aidan, I will. You know, I'm very good with computers."

"I suspect you were not 'very good' the first hour or two."

"No, no, I was not. I was confused and overwhelmed."

"This is much simpler than operating computers, so I'm sure you'll catch on very quickly. Just focus your whole mind on it, understand the nuances, and appreciate the beauty of the process." He smiled, and I felt slightly empowered. "Who knows? Eventually, you may come into the workroom and be happy that this is how you get to spend your time here."

"Perhaps, Aidan," I said, smiling back. "Thanks for the pep talk."

"Ah, well, you're welcome."

"Quick question."

"Yes?"

"What work are you doing behind the screen?"

"Right now, I'm working on two projects. One is proofreading the most recent book I've printed for any print or spacing errors before binding and making the cover. When I finish that, I will be breaking down my next book into printable sections, choosing the typeface and fonts, and calculating the number of quires required to complete the book so I know how much paper I need."

"Quire?"

"Twelve double pages intersected equals twenty-four printed pages. Twenty-four printed pages is a quire. It is important to me—although not to all printers—that the book contains full quires, hence the focus on the font and spacing."

"So, no blank pages?"

"No unintentional blank pages."

I tried to work the math in my head. I could not, so I tried to do it aloud. "That means you would have to—. Oh, my gosh, Aidan! That would take forever! You would have to count the letters of every word on every line and every line on each page."

"More than that, actually, you forgot spaces, but it helps when you know how many characters make a line of type and how many lines you can fit on a page for each typeface—serif or non-serif—"

He abruptly ceased explaining when he saw the puzzled look on my face. "I seem to have lost you. Okay. The easiest comparison is that serif typefaces have the little triangle embellishment on many of the letters, while non-serif typefaces are plainer without extraneous decoration. There are other differences, but we will leave it at that. Once you decide how many lines you want on a page, you can calculate the height of the typeface, and then you will know which font to use: eleven-, twelve-, or fourteen-point. Then, it is necessary to account for the different spacing for italic and bold fonts. Many of the variables between the different typefaces and fonts are minuscule—but they are not nothing and must be considered."

He took a breath and gave me a small smile. "I'm sorry, Helena, I must sound like I'm giving a lecture. You can learn anything on computers, so I'm sure you know all this."

"I know the keys to press and buttons to click to change fonts and typefaces, but I never considered the effect they have on the overall formatting. And you don't sound like a class lecturer; you sound like someone who knows and loves every detail of what he does—and is good at it."

"Well, that is a nice thing to say, but while wordcount and line tallies certainly help, it isn't the most difficult part because most printed books use kerning and—"

"Wait. What the heck is kerning?"

"The space between the letters within a word. It can be as varied as the space between words. My only option for customizing word length is to use either a proportional typeface or non-proportional, also known as a monospace, typeface."

"Proportional typefaces? Okay, you've lost me again. I've been typing all my life; how do I not know this stuff?"

"Proportional typefaces have different widths for the characters, meaning that the space for the letter 'i' takes up less space within a word than an 'm.' A monospace typeface uses the same width for each of the characters. And, as to why you don't know this 'stuff,' I suspect it is because it was too unimportant to be taught in class, or you didn't need to know it in order to get through your assignments and, therefore, you never taught yourself."

He picked up the book I was remaking and opened it to a random page. "Which kind of typeface is this?"

I immediately looked for an 'i' and an 'm' and said, "Proportional."

"Yes. That is why we are using drawers from this side of the cabinet," he said, running his hands over the wooden drawers on the left. "And please do not try lifting these drawers yourself. They are heavy, and unless you want to spend a lot of printing time sorting type back into the appropriate compartments, wait for me to bring whatever you need to the table."

***

I'd like to say I always waited for him, but it would not be the truth. The only redeeming moment of the entire incident was the look on Aidan's face when he saw me sitting on the floor picking up spilled type and resorting them; it was a cross between incredulity and unbridled amusement. He didn't laugh, but then he didn't offer to help either. He only sat down and, for what seemed like days, just watched, correcting my placement of some of the characters, then, after picking the perfectly sorted drawer from the floor, said, "Please do not do this again."

"I won't, I promise," I answered. "I didn't know the drawers were so heavy. You do it so easily."

"Experience is a great—though occasionally painful—teacher."

"Yes, well, I promise I won't do it again."

"Hmmm, so you say." He set the drawer on the table. "If I'm not here, and you need something, just say 'Aidan.' You needn't call or yell. Sound carries quite well in curved space." He looked at me for a moment. "And, unlike others currently occupying the same space, I answer to *my* name."

"Aidan, how many times do I have to say I'm sorry for damaging your book?"

"I don't know yet."

Several practice sheets later, Aidan was standing next to me, pointing out the few remaining spacing errors, when, without warning, I had to sit down. Setting the composing slate on the table, I looked up.

"I'm sorry, Aidan. I need to rest."

"How is that possible? Are you also hungry or thirsty? Do you require toilet facilities?"

"No, but I need to rest my mind," I said, lightly rubbing my forehead. "How long have I been working?"

"Only about twenty Earth hours."

"Twenty? . . . Well, that explains it."

"Explains what?"

"The reason why I feel so tired."

"I have neither bed, nor cot, nor pillow here. As you know, Helena, I wasn't expecting a visitor."

"It's okay, I'll just lie down on the floor."

"If you wish."

***

As he watched, she walked a few steps away from the worktable and lay down on the floor. Tucking the ends of her shirt around her knees, she curled up with her back against the curve of the wall and, despite the light overhead, was asleep within minutes. He turned away and began stacking the paper she would need for the next few pages. Then, as he was sorting the type back into the drawer, he turned and saw that her face had slipped off her arm onto the floor.

His hands hovered motionless above the type drawer. For the first time, it occurred to him that she might be uncomfortable. He sat down next to her, lifted her into his arms, and her head fell naturally against his shoulder. He felt her breathing. In the silence of the room, her heartbeat sounded like music. Her skin was warm where it touched him. He moved his arm around her and appreciated how the softness of her body felt against the muscles of his own. Unexpectedly, he decided the imperfections that deemed her unworthy of his earlier notice were not as insurmountable as he originally believed.

The short time they had spent together in his "Paradise" had not passed unhappily. Once she'd understood that she wasn't going to be late for work by being here, a sense of calm had descended upon her, and he noted certain elements of natural grace in her movements and a pleasing lilt in the cadence of her voice. She had even made him laugh.

Perhaps if he focused on those qualities instead of the ones she lacked, this punishment would be less arduous for him. For recreating the book was *his* punishment—not hers. Her feelings of guilt had made her docile enough to be convinced that the damage was her fault, but his pride—in his work and his control over this part of the universe—was the real crime.

He was the one who had left the door unlatched, and he was still angry with himself for letting her carelessness provoke him to the point of bringing her into his workshop. He wished he had taken her back into the shop once he realized the book had to be entirely remade, but when her feelings of guilt turned to curiosity, he thought having someone to talk to would be a pleasant diversion and decided to keep her as an apprentice so he could finish more quickly.

He hoped he would not regret it.

Sitting motionless on the floor, he held her as gently as he could and considered the different ways of making the best of this new intrusion into his life. What if he could push her a bit? He could not change her appearance, but intellect had its own beauty. It was clear that teaching her how to make a book was going to be a slower process than he had originally imagined. Perhaps he could use that time, and her apparently unending supply of questions, to broaden her interests to include subjects that appealed to him. It would be worth the effort. An occasional intelligent conversation would make working with her more bearable. Separate workspaces had helped, but his attentiveness to her progress made her a greater distraction to him than he was to her.

While waiting for her to awaken, he studied the austerity of his workshop and imagined a few minor alterations to make it more comfortable for both of them.

When her eyes began to flutter, he eased from beneath her and returned to the worktable.

She pulled herself to a sitting position and looked around as though she had forgotten where she was, then shook her head for a moment. Cupping her chin in her hand and resting her elbow on her knee, she looked up at him.

"Did I sleep long?"

"I thought so, but if you feel better, it does not matter. I do, however, regret that I was unaware of your fatigue. I will try to pay closer attention. You do feel better, don't you?"

"I'm not tired anymore."

"Good. Do you need anything else?"

"No, but I've been thinking."

"In the last two minutes?"

"No, before I fell asleep."

"About?"

"Well, Aidan, this is, um, lovely and all, but what if I want to leave?"

"Before you've finished your work?"

"Yes. It occurs to me that everything will be really strange if I'm away for a long time. I know I'll be the same, but won't everything else be different?"

He was quiet for a few moments, then said, "I thought you understood, but apparently, I was mistaken, so I shall try again." He sat in the chair and faced me. "Helena, for the fourth, or possibly fifth, time we've had this conversation, time does not exist in this space. I don't know how to say it any simpler than that. The hands on the clock above the door will not advance until we have returned to the shop, regardless of how long you are in the scriptorium. As far as the Earth world is concerned, it is still 12:45 and, for as long as you are here, that will not change. No one is missing you."

"I understand that, but . . . Wait a minute." She looked down for a moment, then lifted her head. "No one is missing me," she repeated slowly, "for as long as I'm in here."

"That is correct. No one knows you are gone."

"Right. No one knows." At first, she laughed softly to herself, then, standing, she laughed louder with a kind of joy. "Aidan, I'm free," she said.

"Hardly. You promised to stay and remake my book."

"Yes, but that is just between you and me. The rest of my world is now just a concept, not a reality. Nothing I do here will be weighed, measured, or judged by anyone other than your less-than-stellar expectations; there is no one else within these lovely flowing walls whose approval matters."

She caught a glimpse of uncertainty on his face. "Don't you understand? I have no social commitments to fulfill or bills to pay. I have no parents or friends to judge everything I do and every word I say. No roommates, no officemates, no pets, no shopping for dinner. I don't have to worry every minute about what someone is going to ask of me. I can explore who I am, timelessly and freely. Oh, Aidan, you've stopped time for me, and I can finally breathe." She stretched out her arms as though trying to embrace all that surrounded her. "Thank you for letting me share your corner of Heaven."

Slightly out of breath, she sat down in her chair opposite him and smiled. She looked different. Whether the change was from sleeping or her newfound inner joy was immaterial. The shadows had disappeared from beneath her eyes; her smile held no reluctance. The suppressed loveliness that hovered at the contours of her face now softened the edges of her cheekbones and jaw. Her eyes were luminous, large, and clear. He would have happily explained it another half-dozen times to watch the realization of her "timeless freedom" transform her from a common bug to a resplendent butterfly.

Although he approved of her new beauty, he kept her metamorphosis a secret pleasure that he would never share—not even with her.

***

I woke up alone.

Stealthily, and listening every moment for Aidan's footsteps, I walked toward the first of the three doors on the right side of the hallway. I glanced down the curve of the corridor. Not seeing anyone or hearing a sound, and believing I was quite alone, I grasped the handle and slowly opened the door to the forbidden room.

Unlike the unending light in the workroom, this room was dark and shadowy; it was cooler, too. Almost cold. Six tables were lined up in pairs, covered with white sheets. Two or three seemed to be protecting something substantial, and, on the other tables, the sheets were flat and smooth. Curious and wondering if they covered books in progress or printing supplies, I walked to the closest table and lifted the sheet. It was a man's face. I uncovered another and found a different face. Jerking the cloth from the table, I saw the body, still and cold. Filled with dread, I knew one of the empty tables was waiting for me. Screaming, I ran for the door I could no longer find.

***

Someone was tapping my face. "Helena, wake up, Helena, you're screaming—"

86

I jumped up and moved away from him. "That room," I pointed, "that room you won't let me enter; I know what's in there. I want to go home. I, I must leave now! I won't stay another minute."

"That room? Is that why you were screaming? What do you think is in there?"

"I know what's in there! Bodies, dead bodies of your other 'apprentices'! And I won't be one of them!"

"You are wrong, Helena," he said calmly.

He reached for my hand, but I backed away. "Okay," he said, "just follow me."

I didn't move.

Without waiting, he walked to the door and opened it. The room was as bright as the workroom, and from where I was standing, I could see that there were no empty tables in the room but tables holding scraps of linen and stacks of paper, screens, a wooden press, and a large vat. Keeping him at a distance, I walked as close to the doorway as I dared. I didn't know much about printing presses, but I knew paper-making equipment when I saw it.

"Why did you forbid me to go in there?"

"Some of the chemicals in this room are toxic, especially if spilled or inhaled. Most of them are in unmarked bottles or containers, and I didn't want anything to hurt you. Besides, I told you that there was enough paper already made, so there is no reason for you to come in here. This is my *home*, such as it is, not yours to wander about."

He closed the door.

"I think, Helena, that all our discussions about Heaven, spirits, and Hell, together with some of Miss Alcott's more lurid tales told through Jo's imagination, caused you to have a bad dream." He looked wistful for a moment. "I'm sorry our conversations have not been more varied. Perhaps we should set aside those topics for a while and search for new ones."

"Aidan, I'm sorry. I feel so wretched. Not only for what I accused you of, and I am sorry, truly sorry, for that, but I'm beginning to feel so unlike myself. Slightly dizzy and scattered."

"I've noticed that your work, while consistently improving, has become less efficient of late." He looked at me, and it felt like he was mentally checking my appearance, one millimeter at a time.

***

She was right, he thought. Although he had painstakingly created the perfect environment for her survival, it was obvious something was wrong. She was fading like a flower.

Just . . . like . . . a . . . flower.

He closed the door to the paper-making room and said, "May I approach you?"

"Y-yes."

"Hold out your arm, please. I promise I won't hurt you."

She did as he asked, and he pushed back the sleeve of her smock. After pinching the skin of her arm, he raised his hand to touch her hair. "May I?"

She nodded.

He felt the dryness of her hair, lowered his hand, and stepped back.

"You're dehydrated," he said. "Your body isn't changing, but the lack of humidity in the air is evaporating the moisture from your skin."

"But I'm not thirsty."

"No, but your body is," he said. He looked concerned for a few moments, then smiled. "I think I may have an answer. Why don't you sit down and, when you feel better, start composing the next page until I return?"

"I can do that," she said.

***

He turned toward the corridor. When I could no longer hear his footsteps, I walked over and reopened the door. It was precisely the same as before: the bright light, stacks of paper, and two long tables fitted together in an L-shape. Linen, cotton, and a stack of scrap paper, which I recognized as the remnants of my error-filled pages, were stacked neatly on one side. On the other side of the table, I saw framed screens, deckled paper, layers of felt, and a large wooden press. All the supplies were laid out in perfect sequence. On the table closest to the vat, with its hand-cranked beater, stood several bottles that appeared to contain lime, bleach, and boric acid, but I wasn't sure because, as he said, there were no labels. I stood for a moment, admiring the simplicity and perfection of the process. Making paper was something I had done on a much smaller craft-sized scale. I closed the door, wishing I could have made the paper I needed. Sighing in wonder at my stupid imagination or dream or whatever it was, I went back to the printer table and began pulling the letters and spacers for the next page.

I was almost finished composing the practice draft when Aidan walked into the workroom, smiling happily. Not bothering to ask my permission this time, he took my hand. "I can't wait to show you this!" he said, leading me down the hallway.

A blue wavering light emanated from an alcove. "There it is," he said, letting go of my hand.

I followed the light down a short spiral pathway and stopped when I saw the waterfall. Tall and majestic, the cascading water splashed almost soundlessly into a crystal-clear pool encircled by stones, plants, and flowers. Soft lights, shimmering from hidden places between the stones, illuminated the water's edge. Surrounded by several boulders of different heights, the waterfall was situated at the far end, where the water became darker and deeper. A gentle, beach-like slope leading into those depths started where I stood.

I knew Aidan was behind me, and I turned toward him. "It's a garden!" I said, unable to keep the excitement from my voice. "How did you do this? It's beautiful."

"Matter in the fourth dimension can be manipulated if the elements are naturally occurring and kept simple. That you believe it is beautiful is just a gift."

"Thank you."

"You're welcome. Stay until you feel better; refreshed, I think, is the best word to use. I brought you a dry shirt, and so, I guess I'll leave you here. "

"You're not staying?"

"Do you want me to stay?" He said, barely suppressing the surprise in his voice.

"Of course! We need to buddy up."

"Do what?"

"You know, swim in pairs to keep each other from drowning."

"That is very considerate of you, but I regret I do not have swimming clothes."

"Well, neither do I, but if we keep our shirts on, it would be okay. If I'm dehydrated, you might be, too. And besides, we need to find other topics of conversation."

"All right. I'll go get us both some dry clothes," he said, walking away.

***

Once he was out of her line of sight, Aidan smothered his laughter at the thought of *her* saving *him* from drowning! Then, reflecting on the depth of her generosity and naïveté, he smiled and shook his head. The truth of who he was had not yet seemed to dawn on her, yet he was glad of it. The longer he kept to her expectations of him, the longer she would stay. He wouldn't even try to seduce her; he would wait until she wanted him. *It was only a matter of time*, he thought, and he—more than any creature in the seven realms—had all the time in the world.

***

Aidan sat on the edge of the pool and watched as I dived into the water. Unused to such scrutiny—even as disinterested as he seemed to be—I watched him out of the corner of my eyes as I swam, floated, and explored.

Feeling I should get to know him better if we were going to spend so much time together, I thought I'd ask some questions my dream had raised. The more I knew about him, the easier it would be to live with him.

"*Live with him*!" I laughed to myself. *As if.*

I swam over to where he sat and put my arms on the ledge as my body and legs were still immersed in the fresh, cool water, and looked up at him.

"Aidan, you said you are a spirit—"

"Mostly spirit. I have a body of flesh like you."

"Okay, fine. When you were in your 'mostly spirit' state, did you ever go to Hell?"

"I thought we were not going to have any more of these conversations. Are you sure you don't want to discuss the flowers I chose for the garden?"

"I'm sure we'll get to that, but I want to understand more about you." I paused, but he didn't respond. "Well, did you?"

He sighed. "Okay, we'll have this conversation, but if you start getting nightmares, you will only have yourself to blame." He looked at me until I nodded.

"Of course," he said. "Everyone goes to Hades first."

"Wait, what? Everyone goes to Hell?"

"That is not what I said. Hades is not the same as Hell. It's a mercy, really. Think about it. If everyone went to Heaven first, the despair of then being sent to Hell would make an existence eternally without redemption or hope unbearable. Separation from God is the worst punishment imaginable, and to glimpse what an eternity with God looks and feels like and then to lose that forever is cruel. God is just—not cruel. So, spirits go to Hades, then ascend to Heaven or descend into Hell."

"Are there any other differences between Heaven and Hell besides being separated from or in the presence of God?"

"You mean like fire and brimstone and devils with pitchforks?"

"Well, ..."

He almost laughed. "There is fire, but it is used for light. The only natural light in any of the realms is from God's love, so Hell is dark. There is no brimstone; there is only the smell of smoke from the torches—not sulfur. And as far as the popular image of devils with pitchforks, such beings are totally unnecessary because there is no escape. If you are in Hell, you are in Hell."

"So, no one is tortured?"

"Torture comes in many different forms," he said. "In Hell, it's the noise. There is endless talking in Hell. Heaven is quiet; everyone is soft-spoken and speaks the same language. In Hell, everyone speaks a different language, so the spirits are always looking for another spirit who understands them. They move around, constantly listening for words they recognize, or they mumble, or even sometimes yell, random words to see if anyone recognizes what they are saying. No one can hear you in hell because the inhabitants are listening so intently through the constant collision of sounds for a word or two that they know that they do not hear the words they don't understand."

"Do they ever find another spirit that understands them?"

"Sometimes, but it is rare. There are billions of spirits, all milling around, so it's hard to find someone who understands your specific language. And much depends on the spirit who does understand you—this is Hell, remember? It is not always possible to like the spirit whose language you understand."

"So, the spirits in Hell are not only separated from God; they are also separated from each other," she said with a shudder.

"Yes," he answered, "it's Hell."

"But you know, I think that happens everywhere, even here on Earth, even if there isn't a language barrier," I said. "Finding someone who understands you and that you can care for is a risky proposition here, too."

"Yes. Hell is what you—alone—can make of it; Heaven is what you can make of it together with love and respect. The Earth world, it seems, can go either way."

He smiled and tilted his head. "What have you made of your life on Earth, Helena?"

I didn't know where to start. "It's complicated," I answered.

"Complicated? Well, let's simplify the question." He thought for a moment and said, "What about *Little Women?* For instance, do you identify with any of the March girls?

I held out my hands, and he helped me climb out of the pool. I sat next to him and started drying off.

"Well, let me think. I'm not very musical, so definitely not Beth. I love making things—"

"Like books?" he asked, smiling.

"Um, well, I like making them now," I answered. "But I have no real artistic talent. Certainly, no one would take me to France to study painting, so Amy is out." I thought for another minute. "I tried being a housewife, like Meg, but apparently, I wasn't good at that either, so I guess that leaves Jo. Jo . . . that's me; independent with a love of books."

"Tell me what happened to Meg."

"Nothing much to say. It was quite wonderful—until it wasn't—and then it was over." I sighed, knowing I couldn't avoid saying the next few words. "He found someone else."

"Did you love him?"

"I did, . . . in my own way."

He looked at me quizzically. "And what way was that?"

"I was the right age. I thought he was the right person. I wanted to get my life started. You know, a husband, a home, and," I paused for a moment, "children. As it turned out, I was in love with the idea of that life, not him. He is a kind man, and I appreciated that. I thought what I had to give him was enough and that it would be okay."

"But, according to some of the books I've read, especially those written in the twentieth century, it does not work that way."

"Well, it didn't work for us, so we separated. He found someone else—someone who considers him the center of her life, not just a part of it. It was what he should have had in the beginning. So, now I have no love, no kind man, and no children," I said lightly, not wanting him to feel sorry for me. "You see? Just like Jo, I am footloose and fancy free."

Aidan wasn't deceived. "It was more complicated than that," he admonished.

"Most relationships usually are, but what I said was true."

Aidan nodded. "Do you hate him?"

"No, why would I hate him? I'm glad one of us is happy, even if we couldn't be happy together."

He leaned in my direction. "Look at me, Helena."

I looked into his eyes, so beautifully blue yet so clear. "Why?"

"I want to see if you are telling the truth or if you are being brave."

"And . . .?"

"Both."

"So, among your other talents, you are also a lie detector?"

"Few women can lie convincingly," he said. "Be happy you are not one of them. Men are better at it."

I laughed and said, "No comment."

Sequences

It did not take long for Aidan to notice that the time spent in the water was exactly what she needed. Her skin became soft and recovered its natural resilience, and swimming infused her with both renewed mental and physical energy. Although he congratulated himself on his success, Aidan soon found that in a dimension where time, as a measurement, does not exist, he had to devise a way to track her movements to determine when she needed a hydration immersion, which she referred to as a "dip in the pool," or rest. Waiting for her to show signs of fatigue or dehydration was inefficient because they were not obvious until she started making mistakes. Unwilling to take any chances with her health, he began to observe her work to chart predictable breaks.

As a quire consisted of twenty-four pages, he suggested that she rest at the end of six pages or even fewer if the printing was particularly difficult. When she awoke (usually in his arms), they would walk to the pool. It wasn't long before she began referring to every six pages of the twenty-four-page stint as "day" and her resting time as "night." These terms settled her mind, and the familiar rhythm proved beneficial as she began approaching her work with a sense of purpose. There were no more nightmares, and she was, he was sure of it, beginning to trust him and, maybe, even liked sharing the scriptorium with him. Her presence had also given him an unexpected benefit: an experience he was beginning to enjoy more than he ever anticipated.

The pool was a wonder to him. It was the perfect place to have conversations where he wasn't teaching, and she wasn't occupied with tasks. Although he didn't understand many of her references, he enjoyed exploring her mind and listening to her voice. She was a good swimmer, and he liked watching her glide effortlessly through the water. He considered keeping the pool after she was gone. It would help him remember her, and the body he wore benefited from it as well. He didn't need the garden, though; that was created purely to appeal to her feminine nature.

Something of which he was becoming increasingly aware.

So much so that as an acknowledgment of her hard work in completing her first quire, he introduced her to the resting room he created for her. Initially, he had planned a simple wooden bed, a corner desk, a chair, and a small chest for clean shirts and socks. Then, deciding it was too plain, he added some flowers from the garden and raided the paper-making room for yards of the softest linen for a coverlet and cotton batting for a mattress and pillow. He filtered the light to sunset amethyst and even built a door to give her the illusion of privacy.

When he showed it to her, she hugged him—briefly—and said, "Oh, Aidan, this is too perfect! Now I won't have to sleep on the floor, or you, anymore!" Following her into the room, he watched her twirl with arms outstretched. "This is quite wonderful, you know. I'm so grateful that you took the time to do this."

"I should have done it before," he said. "I'm sorry. I'm not used to having . . . guests."

Leaving her to examine the room, he stood near the door and listened to her soft sighs of delight until he knew from the sound of her breathing that she was asleep. He had not considered, when building this space for her, that she would sleep away from him. He had grown to like holding her while she slept. It gave him a chance to stop—if only for a few minutes—before he went and fixed *most* of the errors she'd made that day. There were fewer all the time now, and he thought that, before too long, he would not have to leave her at all. Her new room, however, altered *his* evening rest as well as hers.

He turned away from her room and walked down a carefully disguised passageway into the dark room of her dream. He placed Aidan's body on one of the empty tables and covered it up. He never understood how the existence of this room entered her subconscious, and was gratified he had moved it to his cache of hidden chambers before her nightmare became a reality. Very few things had the power to distress him, but the thought of her body resting cold and still on one of the tables shook him to his core.

He glanced at the two other bodies under their damp sheets, exactly as their previous owners had left them. Each of them, at one time or the other, had entered his bookstore and tried to rob him. Of course, they had no idea with whom they were dealing, and after he had dispatched their spirits to the world of *their* nightmares, he'd saved the bodies. Cleaning them and dressing them appropriately, he wore them as the mood struck him.

The body he called Aidan, however, did not try to rob him. He'd walked into the bookshop, saying something about a headache and, within minutes, died of an aneurism between historical romance and horror. He remembered standing over the dead man with amazement. He had never been gifted with a perfect, unscarred body. After immediately taking the man into the dark room, he returned to the storefront and waited impatiently for the remainder of the hour to pass. No one came in looking for the body's previous owner, and when the clock chimed one, he locked the door. Randomly choosing a book from the stacks in the front room as his next project, he went beyond the shimmering portal to try on his new clothes. "Aidan" suited him well—both in stature and commonplace appearance—and quickly became his favorite human disguise.

Now, leaving Aidan's body with its limitations in the cold room, he moved between the walls of his fourth-dimensional realm as pure spirit. Invisible and silent, he surrounded her until she rested within him, and the only movements in the room were the gentle rise of her breath and her heart beating in his chest.

***

When she returned to the printing area after their time in the pool at the beginning of the next "day," he handed her the two or three pages he had saved for her to remake. She set them on the table.

"What is it?" he asked.

"I was thinking while I was swimming this morning. Do you mind if I ask you a question?"

"As long as you understand that I am not under any obligation to answer you."

"Um, okay."

"Well?"

"Would it sound terribly rude if I asked what was behind the other two doors?

"Yes, but if it will prevent any further screaming, I'll tell you." He walked over and stood in front of the middle door. "This is my foundry. Sometimes, I have to create tools specific to my needs that require intense heat. It is well-insulated but dangerous. I would appreciate it if your peace of mind does not need confirmation." He pulled a key out of his pocket and put his hand on the door handle. "However, if it does, then please stand as far away as possible so you won't be burned. I only have one flame-resistant suit."

"Why is it locked?"

"So that I do not open it by mistake. I've considered relocating this room further down the hallway for safety purposes, but it is so convenient to my workspace that I have not done so. I am as combustible as you are, and I have learned to be careful." He waited for a moment. "So, do you want me to open it? I'll stand behind the door and do it very quickly. Or you could just stand next to me where the heat from the door can warm you if that will satisfy your curiosity."

***

It sounded possible, but I didn't believe him. No one would keep a furnace so close to piles of paper, key or no key. I walked over and, with obvious disbelief, laid the flat of my right hand against the door. He snatched it away before I could move it. I gasped in shock. The door was not only warm, but it felt like a burning element on a stove.

"What did I just say?" he said, leading me to the sink in the paper-making room and thrusting my hand beneath the cool water. I could not escape the annoyance that showed clearly on his face—or in his voice.

"I said, 'stand next to me,' I did not say touch the door. But you didn't listen. You can't work with your hands in bandages."

"I'm sor—"

"No. Do not say you're sorry for deliberately doing something I asked you not to do. Just, please, pay attention and *listen* to me."

He pulled my hand from under the water and gently dried it with a piece of cotton as he inspected it carefully. Then, unexpectedly, he placed it against his cheek. Nodding to himself, he let go of my hand and said, "We'll keep an eye on it. I don't detect any residual inflammation, so I don't think you will have blisters."

"I regret I did not believe you. It just seemed so impossible."

"In what way does it seem impossible? How can you be any judge of what is—or is not—possible here? Everything within this space is by my design; parts of it have taken centuries to create, some things only a few hours, so—"

"Like the pool?" I interrupted him.

"What?"

100

"Like the pool. You designed and created that wonderful garden and waterfall in the length of time it took me to compose a single page."

"It was the solution to a problem."

"Yes, but you could have thrown a bucket of water over my head or submerged me in a rain barrel, yet you made it beautiful and welcoming."

"This is my home."

"Yes, it is," I said softly. I looked in the direction of the foundry. "What do you make in there?"

"Different things. The few cutting tools need to be kept very sharp, and the iron parts of the printing press must be replaced occasionally."

"Why keep it so hot if you only use it occasionally?"

"The coals are currently banked. It is hot enough right now to cook you, but it is not hot enough to melt or cast iron; for work like that, the ore must be heated to over three thousand degrees."

"Oh, my."

"Yes. So, do you see why it is important to be careful?"

"Yes, Aidan, I do." While I was satisfied that he was no longer angry, I still had one more question. "Um, now that I know what is in the middle door, I'm almost afraid to ask what is behind door number three. A pit of alligators, perhaps?"

The stern expression on his face eased into one of soft laughter. "No, Helena, I have no need for alligators. However, I do need supplies, so there are just boxes in that room. Some with books for the shop, some with clothes, and others hold small supplies. Things that are easier to buy than make. After all, I'd rather make books than shoes."

"I don't suppose you have a spare belt in there?"

"No, why?"

"Aidan, I'm wearing a tent."

"Ah, worried about being out of fashion? Well, we cannot have that."

He walked over to the scrap table and removed a length of linen from the bottom of the pile and tore a long strip from it.

"This is almost a belt," he said, handing it to me.

When I finished tying it around my waist, I pirouetted and asked, "Does this look better?"

"What's the difference?"

"I have a shape!"

"You had a shape before, but I can see the usefulness of keeping the fabric close to your body while you are working."

Smiling to myself, I shook my head. We were returning to the workspace when I suddenly remembered something and pivoted back to the room.

"Wait a minute. You have a sink in here? There wasn't a sink in here yesterday. I know because I wondered how you got water to the vat for mixing."

"There was a faucet here yesterday, but a sink makes water access more efficient, and I thought you might find it useful. See? I added soap to make it easier for you to wash your hands."

"Did you also add a toothbrush, toothpaste, and a hairbrush? Because those things would be useful, too."

He laughed and said, "I'll rummage in the supply room and see what I can find."

"Do you think you could find any ladies' underthings in there?"

"And what would you say if I said, 'Yes, I do'?"

"I'd say, 'I wear a size four.'"

"And I'd say it was closer to a five. Regretfully, however, I do not have any ladies' underthings—or over-things—of any size in my supply room or anywhere else."

"Well, what do you wear?"

"Excuse me?"

"You said I was a guest now, which is several steps up from vandal, and I would like . . . something . . . please."

"I'll see what I can do," he said. After pausing for a moment, he asked, "Would you like to see the boxes behind door number three?"

"No, I believe you," she said with full confidence.

A slight smile played on his lips as he picked up her hand and peered at the fading redness.

"I'm afraid I am going to have to give you a bit of a holiday. Why don't you find a nice book," he said, pointing to the shelves that curved against the wall on the left side of the room, "and rest your hand today."

"Only if you promise we can go for a swim later."

"Whenever you'd like."

***

He found her in her room, propped up on a pillow, reading Jane Austen's *Pride and Prejudice*.

"'It is a truth universally acknowledged—,'" he began quoting.

"'—that a single man in possession of a good fortune, must be in want of a wife,'" she answered.

"How many times have you read that one?" he asked, pointing to the book.

"You don't want to know," she said. "I really prefer *Sense and Sensibility*, although I haven't read it as often."

"It lacks the dynamic tension between the main characters that keeps readers of *Pride and Prejudice* repeatedly enthralled."

She laughed. "You know, sometimes when you talk about books, you sound more like an English lit professor than a printer."

"Well, most printers read, else what's the point?"

"True," she said, then noticed a bag in his hands. "What are you holding?"

"Your guest requests," he said.

Walking to the edge of the bed, he laid them out as he named them. "Toothbrush, toothpaste—and it's the only kind I have, so don't ask for mint flavored. And a comb, I regret we seem to be out of hairbrushes at the moment, and the, um, other things you requested."

***

I looked at the items on the bed. The toiletries were the kind you'd find at any drugstore, and stacked neatly next to them were two unopened packages of men's boxer shorts. White. No pattern, no print, no other solid colors mixed in—just white.

"Thank you, Aidan. This was very kind of you."

"You're welcome," he said, walking nearer to where I was sitting on the bed. "May I see your hand?"

"Of course."

Once again, he pressed it against his face and smiled. "No blisters," he said. "I look forward to seeing you in the workroom after you've rested." Not letting go of my hand, he added, "Time for a swim?"

"Yes!" I said, leaving Miss Elizabeth Bennet and Mr. Darcy to work things out as I followed him to the pool.

***

Aidan was right; there were no blisters on her hand the next morning, and the redness was beginning to fade. Returning to the workroom, she listened patiently as Aidan pointed out the letter, spacing, and margin errors she needed to correct. Once those pages were successfully reprinted, the first quire was perfect.

"Are we finished?" she asked.

"Only with the printing portion. The quire itself still needs attention."

104

Approaching the workspace, he set the pinhole cradle and the awl in front of her.

"Who am I supposed to stab with that?"

Smiling, he said, "It's whom, Helena." Then, looking down at the tools on the table, he asked, "Haven't you ever—in your entire life—wondered how a book is constructed?"

"To be honest, I'd have to say, 'No.' I just assumed it was all glued to the spine."

"I've seen some paperbacks made that way, but that is not how you construct a book meant to last for millennia. And," he continued, "that is what we hope to accomplish here."

"I know. I'll stop asking questions for five minutes so you can explain."

"Five whole minutes?" he said, laughing. "We'll see."

Pointing to the tools on the table, he added, "Before you sew the pages together, they must be punched. The stitching needle is not strong enough to puncture all of the pages at one time."

He sorted the pages in order, then demonstrated the task by folding the first three pages exactly in half and placing the fold into the "V" of the wooden cradle. He fitted the punch template on top of the paper and tilted the template toward her so she could see a line of tiny white dots of the paper showing behind the template. Taking the awl, he pressed it into each of the holes in the template. She nodded at the sound of the crisp paper being pierced, and after he removed the perforated pages, she took the awl from him. He stood over her and watched as she punched the next three pages correctly and then walked away.

"Call me when you're done," he said.

Piercing the last set of pages, she said, "Aidan," only to find him already standing next to her, holding a needle, thread, and a wooden press. "Oh, sorry. I didn't know you were there."

"Obviously."

He set the press on the table. "This press holds the pages together to ensure they do not shift, allowing them to be sewn into a completed quire."

"I was wondering why there was a needle and thread on the table. I didn't know books were sewn."

"Yes. Some are, others are merely pressed, glued, and wrapped. My books are sewn first."

He took the punched pages from her, double-checked the order, and laid them flat into the press. The perforations on the outside fold showed on top. "If you have done this correctly, the sewing only takes a few minutes, but watch carefully; there is a pattern to it. Once you have all the quires sewn individually, you must sew them together as a single unit. If they do not line up perfectly, you get to do the book again."

"How many times did you have to 'do the book again' when you created this book?"

"I was careful and only had to make this book once," he said. "Then, again, this particular volume wasn't my first book." He ran the length of thread through a small cut in a candle to wax it, then moved her chair next to his. "Watch how I sew the pages and knot the thread after each section. Notice that the needle does not puncture the paper at all—it merely guides the thread through the hole. "

She bent close and watched every movement of his hands. He stitched through three holes, knotted the thread, skipped two, stitched three, knotted, skipped two, stitched three, knotted, skipped two, and then knotted the thread at the end of the last three. Clipping the thread, he looked at me. "Do you think you can do this?"

"Yes, I love to sew."

"You want a home and family, and you love to sew? You're a bit of an anachronism, aren't you?"

She thought for a moment and said, "Yes, I like what I like, so I guess I am a little old-fashioned. But I don't mind."

Neither do I, he thought.

Bringing himself back to the present, he picked up the scissors and, clipping the threads, pulled them slowly and carefully from the holes. He handed her the threaded needle and slid the wooden press in her direction. "Your turn," he said, "I'm going to get a fresh ream of paper."

***

I knew every stitch he'd taken, so when he set the paper on the table, I handed him the press.

"Finished already?" he asked.

"Yes, I think I did pretty well."

He took one look at my handiwork and shook his head. Picking up the scissors, he snipped the threads and once again carefully removed them.

"Why did you do that? I know the stitching was perfect."

"You missed the knot on the second set of stitches. Try again."

He walked away. *I can do this,* I said to myself, picking up the needle and thread and starting again.

He removed my second set of stitches. "Too tight," he said. "The pages will buckle as soon as you take them out of the press. Take a deep breath, relax, and try again."

I started over.

With dread, I watched him pick up the scissors for the third time. "If the stitching is this loose, the pages will shift. If that happens, you either have pages out of alignment or you will need to make the holes bigger to accommodate the difference. Neither of which is acceptable. Also, as a slight consideration, if I take these threads out one more time, we may have to reprint these pages."

I looked at him in horror. All the work going forward was bad enough, but going back? *I would be there forever.*

"Yes," he said. "And forever is a very long time."

"Wait a minute—is there something about being in this space that allows you to read my mind?"

"No, but your face is very expressive, and your thoughts are predictable." He opened the drawer and handed me another spool of thread. He smiled in encouragement.

"Try to get it right this time."

I took another deep breath and concentrated. By the fourth set, I had gotten the tension right, remembered to knot the threads between all the sewn sections, and didn't poke any extra holes.

He placed the approved quire into a paper wrapper and into a box to keep it clean. Then, he looked at me and smiled. "Only nineteen more to go."

"One small step for a book, one giant leap for book making."

"Are you paraphrasing Neil Armstrong?"

"Maybe . . . is that who said it?"

I cannot describe the look on his face; it was either one of blatant incredulity, or he believed I was the most hopeless person in the universe. Or both. I decided to change the subject.

"We should celebrate."

"What? What could be better than going on to the next set?"

"Taking a few minutes to enjoy the accomplishment of the first set *before* going on to the next set."

"What do you want to do?"

"I think I'll take a dip."

"But, but we already did that this morning."

"I know. I won't be long, and besides, you don't have to join me if you'd rather not."

I stopped just short of the hallway and turned back. "Aidan, could I have about five feet of linen to use for a towel?"

"Of course, I'll bring it to you."

He looked so bewildered at that moment; I felt that if I asked him to fly, he would, indeed, grow wings and try. I smiled into his eyes and turned toward the garden.

"Thank you, Aidan."

***

Her hair bounced on her shoulders, and he followed her into the corridor just in time to see her twirl and skip onto the spiral pathway leading to the pool. He could not understand how her mind worked. Jumping from one thought to another . . . she was exhausting. Another nineteen quires, then binding! What had he been thinking? He could have made three books in the time it took her to make one quire. Still angry at himself because if he had just closed the door, none of this would have happened. He picked up the book she had ruined for all time and slammed it back down on the table. Then he thought of spending the next few minutes in the pool with her. His fingers followed the undamaged edge of the leather and lightly traced the outline of the perfect gold lettering on the cover. He felt Aidan's lips form a smile. *Did it really matter how long it took to make a quire if it was made perfectly?*

No, he thought, *it did not.*

He walked quickly to the paper room, cut two five-foot lengths of linen, and retraced his steps. He arrived just in time to see her drop her shirt on the floor and dive into the pool. Before she came up for air, he'd folded a single towel next to her shirt and left the room.

He continued down the curved wall to his private chambers. There was only so much he could do with this body. He could command the brain as if the arms, legs, face, and fingers were his own, but "Aidan's" body itself was inert. It, like her living body and those in the cold room, was static, incapable of decay or of ever being more than it was when he carried it through the time slip. Because of this stasis, the body he wore was incapable of responding affirmatively to the situation her body had presented so seductively.

Did he even want that kind of physical relationship? *With her?* Originally, he had something a little more ephemeral in mind, a flirtation, perhaps, of wit and wordplay, but she was evolving before his eyes, and he was unsure he could trust himself to get involved that deeply. It was a short step from his mind to his heart and from his heart to obsession. His previous physical relationships rose up to confront him. They had not always worked out well, for women's priorities confused him, and the loss of his children had made him angry, suspicious, and cruel. Centuries of crafting books had taught him patience, and the solitude had tempered his anger, calmed his suspicions, and he had recovered a degree of kindness. However, the years spent in the scriptorium had not altered his past.

Despite his feelings of uncertainty and regrettable memories, he could not ignore the fact that she clearly expected something more from Aidan. *Of course she did,* he thought grimly; *she was alive.*

And she clearly thought Aidan was alive, and that wasn't part of his plan at all.

***

She smiled at him when she returned to the workroom. He was waiting for her at the table and handed her the book. She gently turned the pages, looking for her next printing assignment.

He spoke first. "I regret I missed our celebration."

"That's not all you missed."

"Well, yes. I realized I wasn't appropriately dressed for the occasion."

"Did I embarrass you?"

"No, I do not embarrass easily. I didn't wish to embarrass you."

"In what way?"

"By refusing your unspoken invitation."

"But didn't you do that anyway?"

"No, my absence implied many things . . . I *said* nothing."

"What didn't you say, Aidan?" Her voice was so low it was almost a whisper.

"That such acceptance is beyond the limits of this, um, my body."

"Are you ill?"

He could not miss her sudden change in tone from sassy to almost sounding as if she cared. He quickly decided to change his story.

"Not any longer, " he said gravely. "A small aneurysm several years ago caused a stroke. I've regained full control of my limbs and digits, and even my facial features have returned to me. But despite this progress, not everything works as well as it once did."

"Do you smoke?"

He made a sudden sound between a choke and laughter. "What?"

"I read somewhere that smoking cigarettes can cause strokes. I just asked in case, you know, if you did, you could stop and perhaps not have another stroke."

"No, I don't smoke cigarettes—and before you ask—I don't smoke anything else."

Smiling to offset the smugness of her tone, she said, "Well, then, perhaps it is a matter of motivation."

Aidan had endured enough of this banter. It was pointless, and her attempts at seduction were clumsy at best and cloying at worst. No longer a distraction, she was becoming intrusive. Suddenly, he wanted her gone; he had work to do. His face became stern and forbidding.

"Do you think you are the only woman I've known?"

"No, but I am the only woman here."

"As a distraction, Helena, not as a plaything."

"A distraction?"

"Yes. I don't need your help to make this book. In fact, it would already be finished if not for your lack of finesse. However, since I've made this book once, I thought—for a brief moment— that it would be interesting to have someone to whom I could teach book printing in order to alleviate the utter boredom of recreating something I already know by heart."

"That is a lot of work to go through just for a distraction, Aidan. Do you want me to leave?"

She said it so calmly that he realized he was about three words away from losing her. He bit back his angry retort and said evenly, "No, I want you to stay. I'm just trying to say that I created the garden and the pool for you. You may swim in it however you wish. I have come to enjoy swimming as well. If you prefer your privacy to sharing it with me, I understand. I will look for a small area where I can design my own." He paused at the thought of how lonely that would be and sighed. "That will, of course, make our conversations during our celebratory breaks . . . difficult . . . but it is your choice."

"It's more fun when you're there. I'll wear my shirt, Aidan."

"As will I, Helena, and thank you."

She nodded and wiped her eyes on her sleeve.

"Is the light too bright in here?" he asked.

"No," she sniffed quietly. "It's just that I've been looking for someone for a long time—I thought he might be you. I'm sorry I was so blatant about it." She looked at him and smiled crookedly. "No finesse."

She had never appeared so helplessly human. As vulnerable as she was at that moment, he knew he could do anything he liked to her—or make her do anything he liked, but no. As he had said earlier, she was not a plaything. Realizing now that he had to give her back to herself at some point, he abandoned his plan of slow seduction. *Why make it harder for either of them to let go?*

"As nice as it sounds, Helena, I am not your 'someone,'" he said in his softest voice. "Let's get back on task. I shall teach, and you will learn, and somewhere along the way, perhaps we will become friends. Is that all right with you?"

His conciliatory tone seemed to have worked. Her smile touched her eyes and banished her tears. "Yes, that sounds perfect, Aidan."

Looking down at the open book, she said, "Can you bring the type compartments to the table, please? I'd like to get started on composing the next page.

He did as she asked and then brought the capital letters for the chapter title that he knew she would need as well.

***

Rather than focus on the drama of the afternoon, I just wanted to keep working. After all, I had a life that was waiting for me on the other side of the faded blue door.

"Aidan, I won't change in here? No matter how long I stay?"

"I never said that. I said your body would not change. I have every hope that your mind may change, acquiring a bit of knowledge and wisdom, perhaps, from the things I am teaching you."

"Perhaps. But that doesn't answer my question. For instance, has your body changed?"

"No, it is static flesh, like yours."

"Then that explains why you stay in here so much."

"Excuse me?"

"You don't age. So, the longer you stay in here, the longer you will live. For instance, you look around thirty-five, but how old are you, really?"

"Older than that."

"Well . . .?"

"I don't know exactly how old I am. After all, age isn't a fourth-dimensional concept. However, if we consider that Johannes Gutenberg invented the movable type printing press and printed his Bible in the middle of the 15th century, and we are now in the first half of the 21st century, I am definitely older than thirty-five."

A few minutes later, I shook my head. "That would mean that you are approximately five hundred and fifty years old."

"As I said, I'm older than that, but for argument's sake, let's say I only age during the one hour a year I spend in the bookshop. The rest of the time, I am in here. So, five hundred and fifty years is only five hundred and fifty hours, which works out to about twenty-two or twenty-three Earth days over the last half millennium. But it's more than that because I could not make these books available until I learned to create them. That meant several years spent practicing in here and additional time in the Earth world observing to update my skills as technology advanced. All in all, I'd say I've aged about ten years since I started making books."

"And the rest of that time, you've been in here alone, just making books?"

"Oh, no! I've spent all that time in here alone making gloriously perfect books!"

"May I look at the other books you've done?"

"May I offer you a face mask and tie your hands behind your back?"

"Certainly not!"

"Well, then, certainly not."

"But I will be very careful."

"I see. Have your feelings changed about the mask and wrist ties?"

"No."

"Well, then, no."

"You don't trust me?"

"Given our current situation, would you trust you?"

"Can we compromise with gloves?"

"I don't have gloves."

"I could put socks over my hands."

"I'm not discussing this subject further unless you are willing to accept my terms."

I squinched up my eyes at him. "Grrrr."

He was sitting in front of me, his long legs stretched out between us. At that moment, he leaned in toward me.

"Did you just *growl* at me?"

"Maybe a little . . . just pretending, of course."

"Tell me, Helena, would you like me to growl at you?"

Although his expression did not change, his eyes grew darker, and there was a sensuality in his voice I had never heard before. It sounded deeper, as though he really could growl, and my heart caught in my throat. "No, Aidan. I'm quite sure you would scare the life out of me."

"Not quite," he said. "It would be a soft growl."

"No, thank you. No mask, no wrist ties, no growls, and I promise, no more stupid requests. Deal?"

"It would make our time together simpler," he said, leaning back in his chair, "so, yes. Deal."

Then he laughed softly as though he had been teasing me, but I had seen his eyes, heard the warning in his voice, and I knew, from my visceral reaction, that he was deadly serious. Not only could he growl, but I was also fairly certain he could bite.

As we worked on the book together, I began to get many things right—never the first time and often not the fifth—but I was getting a feel and a liking for the work. However, as I learned, any mistake was time-consuming. All the gold lettering on the error-filled pages had to be scraped off and collected in a shallow bowl for remelting. The letters, words, and phrases that fell into the dish, connected and complete, stared up at me not only as a waste of resources but also as proof of my lack of expertise.

I was slow to understand that even in a place where time does not exist as a construct, the states of past, present, and future—by their essence—embody a sense of time. These words did not disappear from my vocabulary. A limitless now is not unchanging. There are still goals and tasks at every moment, even if the "moment" itself cannot be marked. Just because time is not a burden, has no reference, and cannot be measured, does not mean that it stands still or is insubstantial.

Slowly, very slowly in some instances, the quires were printed and sewn, and the wrapped stack of completed book segments kept safe in Aidan's box grew higher.

On the day I took the last stitch in the tenth quire, I was about to call him, but when I looked up, he was standing next to me, watching me knot the last thread.

He looked at it carefully, nodded, and took it out of the press. Folding, then wrapping the finished quire, he placed the pages in the box. Closing the lid quietly, he looked at me. "You are halfway through the printing, Helena. Congratulations. You've improved—gradually—and I'm quite proud of you."

"Well, I promised."

"Is there anything you'd like to do . . . a celebratory swim, perhaps?

"Sounds like a plan," I said, smiling. "I'll grab the towels and meet you there."

***

Arriving at the garden first, Aidan added some new flowers and adjusted the lights to warm the room.

She stopped at the edge of the pool. "Wow! You changed it. Looks great."

"I just wanted it to look a little more like the summers you're used to. I'm glad you like it."

Without another word, she dove into the deep end of the pool, and he immediately followed her. Throughout their swim, he noticed she was quiet and seemed preoccupied. It was not like her to be quiet if something was on her mind—or at any other time. After a few more minutes of silence, he got out of the pool and picked up a towel. She swam over to where he was sitting.

"Is there something wrong with the pool?" he asked.

"No, it's perfect."

Another moment of silence was more than he could bear. He reached over and picked one of the pink roses. Handing it to her, he asked, "A flower for your thoughts?"

"It's supposed to be a penny."

"Yes, but I seem to have more flowers than pennies today."

She took the flower and breathed in its fragrance. Sighing, she looked up at him, her eyes wide like a child.

"Aidan, do you think you'll ever go back to Heaven?"

"Perhaps, if I ever find something there I want more than the knowledge I can find here."

"What do you think that might be?"

"I can't imagine. As you can see, I am still here."

"What do you miss most?"

"There are some spirits in Heaven that I miss, but not enough to give this up. They will still be there when I return."

"And God?"

"God, the Creator, is everywhere. Even in Hell. His divine patience is as eternal as His love." He thought for a moment and then looked up at me and smiled. "What I miss most is what we are doing now."

"I'm confused. Do you mean swimming or making books?"

"No. I miss conversation. Discourse. The melodious and free sharing of thoughts, experiences, and discoveries. I miss the harmony of like minds and the peace of not having to explain everything to have my meaning understood. As I told you, in Hell, there is no conversation—no sharing of ideas or knowledge. Just a cacophony of random utterances that no one listens to or can understand."

"Except for that one other spirit, right? The one who can understand—if only a little? It's something to hope for . . . something to build on."

He looked at her for a long and solemn moment. "Did you ever read Dante?" he asked.

"Why, yes, in college. Have you?"

"The third book I made—or rather, the third, fourth, and fifth books I made."

She smiled. "So, there are a lot of spirits in Heaven who want to read Dante, are there? I would have never expected that."

"Curiosity, my dear, does not end with death, or I would still be in Heaven. But, of course, *The Paradiso* is read most often. But more to the point, what did you notice about *The Inferno* that was, say, different than in *The Purgatorio?*"

He watched her face as she thought about it.

"Spirits in Purgatory still have hope of Heaven—there is no hope in Hell," she said slowly.

"Exactly right," he said. "No hope, no miracles, and no happy endings."

"So, the hope of finding someone is a lie?"

"It is more than that," he said, "it is a form of passive torture." He paused, wondering how much he could tell her and what she would do with the information, but since caution was never his defining characteristic, he decided to continue. "Strangely enough, the spirits cling to this possibility as though it is a promise while ignoring the greatest promise. All they need to do is accept the love of God, who understands all languages. But few reach that realization. Preferring to wander in their fear of a retribution they are already living."

"So, Dante was right?"

"In some ways, yes, but the vividness of Dante's poetry was colored by his desire for revenge on a world that had taken from him everything he loved."

She looked deep in thought and made no response.

"God is just," he said, touching her hand for attention, "not vengeful. Most people have too many—and too varied—sins to be eternally punished for only one."

He smiled in quiet thought. "I liked making those books. Dante was a fine poet, a genius in structure, and he knew exactly what he was going to write and how it would be written before he began, but his pen was dipped in ink distilled from pain and longing. He was imaginative and meticulous, but his *Divine Comedy* was more allegory—and wishful thinking—than true vision."

"Perhaps," she said, "but Heaven was Heaven to Dante not only because of the presence of God and the celestial spheres but also because Beatrice was there. Would he have so ardently sought Paradise if she hadn't taken his hand?"

"No, he would have dreamt alone in the dark wood and, in the morning, walked away."

"So, she made all the difference."

"No, his love and desire for her made all the difference."

She smiled and said softly, "It always does."

She reached her arm toward him, and he helped her out of the pool. She didn't move away immediately; she just took the towel from him and, placing both hands on his shoulders, stood on her toes and kissed his cheek.

"See you in a few minutes."

He put his fingers where she'd kissed him and watched her walk away, noticing that the set of her head and her walk had an air of confidence and elegance she had not possessed when she left the workroom only an hour before.

***

Even though I was moving timelessly through space, my work developed its own rhythm. Every day I spent printing was usually followed by at least half that time removing the gold from the less-than-perfect pages. Luckily, scraping the letters was not difficult, merely repetitive after the first couple of lines, and one day, although I was not aware of it, I began singing.

There I was, scraping away, when a shadow fell over my work. I didn't look up. "Good morning, Aidan."

"It isn't morning, Helena. There is no sun, no seasons, no eventides—"

"I know, but it feels like morning."

"Is that why you were singing?"

"Was I singing?"

"Yes. Obviously."

"Did it bother you? Was I terribly off-key?"

"No. I just have not heard anyone sing in a long time. And no, you have an adequate voice."

I looked up at him and smiled. "Thanks a lot! Why don't you sing something?"

His face lost all expression. "I don't sing anymore," he said, walking toward the paper-making room. "But you can," he added over his shoulder, "if you wish."

***

I was still scraping when he came back. Although he didn't say anything, he seemed exasperated at my slowness. To give him something else to think about, I asked, "Have you always made books or worked in a bookstore?"

120

He sat down in the chair across from me and crossed his arms.

"Yes and no," he said. "After a couple of centuries of crafting and refining my books, equipment, and technique, I became interested in film. When videos became available, I created a combination video/bookstore. A few years passed, and I realized most of the movies I liked were based on books I had already read. As you may guess, movies cannot be transported; they are all noise: music in the background, sound effects, and overlapping voices that distract and distort the dialogue. I also felt that focusing on video was pulling me away from my primary purpose. Books are so much better because the reader decides the music, the intonation, and the actual sound that exists beyond the word 'said.'"

I nodded my head above the falling flakes of gold. "I totally agree. Whenever I find out that a movie I like is based on a book or short story, I almost always want to read it because films usually leave so much out, which is probably the reason I'm not always eager to see a movie based on something I've read . . . especially if I've liked it."

"That's because the mind of the reader and writer are directly linked through the words. No other mind or vision interferes with the reader's interpretation or mental translation. Unlike a film, of course, that has been filtered through the layers of decision—or indecision—by the screenwriter, director, actors, and film editor, all of whom have direct input into the finished product. When you go through that many minds to create a film from a book, sometimes the only thing that isn't discarded is the title."

He leaned forward. Picking up the last error-filled page and another knife, he began scraping. Seeing this, I seized the opportunity to ask another question that kept popping up in my mind.

"But, Aidan, the words we are using for this book are in English—does everyone in Heaven understand English?"

"Many of the books here are not in English, but it is irrelevant whether the spirits can understand that or any other Earth language. The words transcend those printed here and rise as concepts and ideas that are absorbed into the mind of the spirit. If we were in Rome, for example, the books could be written in English, Latin, or Italian. Although it technically doesn't matter, the printed language I use wholly relies on the original source of the text without any necessary translation. *Comprende, no?*"

Seeing the confusion on my face, he added, "You don't speak Italian?"

"Um, no, I—"

"Just a little Spanish and French, like most American schoolgirls. Don't tell me; I already know. You wanted to learn French, but you were told Spanish was more practical, so you did not learn very much of either one."

"How did you know that?"

"It's not an original story—and, by the way, neither is *Little Women*, but we must get back to that particular task. Are you finished scraping yet?" he asked, setting aside the perfectly cleaned page and the knife.

"Almost. How many languages do you speak?"

"As many as are necessary for my work. The exact number isn't something I think about."

"Can you teach me to speak Italian?"

"I could, but I am teaching you to make books at the moment, and I can tell from here that you've left flakes of gold on the last two pages. Take them out of the pile and finish them properly, *per favore.*"

I wish I could say that I thought of something impressive to say, but I didn't—not even in English—so I just smiled and took the two pages back. He was right, of course. There were still tiny flakes of gold sparkling against the white paper that I had totally missed.

To keep him distracted for the next several minutes while I finished those pages before I could start composing the next page, I said, "I know this is probably not a conversation you want to continue, but is there anything that the spirits in Heaven and Hell have in common?"

"I am open to all topics of conversation, Helena," he said, leaning back in his chair. "To answer this one, yes, there is one common thread that runs through all the spirits wherever they are: they all made permanent decisions based on temporary emotions. Many spirits make good decisions—but too many make bad ones."

"But wait, aren't all emotions temporary?"

"Yes."

"Then aren't we—meaning the entire human race—basically doomed?"

"Not at all, or Heaven would be an empty space. However, if you are asking me if the fate of all living humans is at the mercy of their actions, then yes."

"Seems unfair. Everyone makes mistakes."

"It's the free will thing. In every moment of your existence, you get to choose to be good or to be bad. To help or to hurt. To show mercy or to be cruel. But the most important of these decisions is that you can either freely accept the love of the Creator and treat his creations—the planet, other people, animals—with respect and care, or . . . not. No one is sent to Hell who has not chosen to be there."

"I'm not sure that's true because there are always extenuating circumstances—not every rule applies to every person—but it's an interesting perspective."

"If that is what you think, I will accept your judgment. I know the futility of trying to convince people of anything they aren't ready to believe."

Without another word, he stood and walked away from the worktable to his desk behind the screen.

***

"Interesting perspective!"

This was not a discussion about a random philosophical question; this was about the rest of her existence! He hoped she would never hear the screams of the spirits condemned to Hell. The begging, bargaining, and unending anger and rage that keep them there for all time. For centuries, he tried to explain—to try to make them understand—how easy it was to leave, but his voice was lost in the chorus of trillions of others, and no one could comprehend what he was saying. The longer he tried to convince them, the more like them he became. Retreating to the House of Hades to preserve what little divinity that remained to him, he was allowed to create this space. *God is great, and his mercy is everlasting,* he thought with gratitude.

But *her*. He didn't want that darkness for her. However, he knew from sad experience that you cannot rescue someone who does not wish to be saved.

***

Printing seemed to get easier after the tenth quire. I could read the type backward without pausing to sound out the words. The punctuation, although not correct by current grammar standards, had its own style and soon became predictable. As the end of the printing portion of the project drew near, I felt I was mastering a skill that I had once thought impossible.

Another thing happened, too. As Aidan predicted, I found myself looking forward to coming into the workroom because even though we still had our occasional differences and difficulties, I was always curious to learn what he was going to teach me that day.

Then, just like that, the last page was printed and the last quire sewn. I put down my needle and handed him the stitched and folded pages.

"Twenty quires done! Excellent work! Tomorrow, we can go on to the next step," he said, packing the newly finished quire away in the box.

When I didn't answer, he looked at me. "Helena," he said, smiling, "what are you thinking? You seem a million light years away."

I stretched my arms out and arched my spine. Settling back into the chair, I said, "That's great! I think it's time for a dip."

"That sounds good to me, too, but you didn't answer my question."

I tilted my head. "Oh, sorry, I was just wondering what I would be doing now if I hadn't stepped into your shop."

"What do you mean?" he asked abruptly.

"Only that I was wondering what would be going on in my life if the blue door hadn't opened."

"I see. Are you looking forward to returning to the Earth world?"

"Yes, eventually. It's where my life is."

***

He said nothing else and was unusually quiet during their swim in the garden. She didn't seem to mind as she luxuriated in the loveliness of the waterfall and flowers he had created for her. Keeping to the deeper end, he watched her, but it wasn't long before the echo of her words eclipsed even that pleasure, and he couldn't look at her any longer. Without saying goodnight, he got out of the pool and left.

Pacing in his chamber, he could not shake her words from his mind. *She's thinking about leaving because she wants to leave,* he thought. *Of course she does! What is here for her but constant work, few breaks, limited conversations, and no real rewards? Of course, she wants to leave . . . me.* He could feel his temperature rising and quickly exited Aidan's body before damaging it.

There were few rules to his existence, but she had not come of her own volition and only agreed to stay out of guilt. Under those conditions, he could not take advantage of her innocence, and he could not keep her. Regardless of his growing admiration for her, he wasn't going to spend the rest of her presence in *his* workroom listening to her wonder about what was going on in *her* Earth world while surreptitiously wishing she had never walked into his shop.

He understood his emotional limitations as well as he understood Aidan's physical limitations, and he knew he could not bear to live with her if he had to listen to her speculative imaginings, casual regrets, and impatient longings to return.

Better to let her go. They had finished the printing, and he knew that, given the rate of her learning curve, the endpapers, binding process, and cover could easily take as long as the printing. His existence would be easier—and he would get more work done—without her. A few minutes later, he made up his mind. He would tell her that she did not have to stay any longer.

He looked at Aidan's body stretched across the floor and waited until his mind settled before sliding his spirit back into it. But borrowed flesh and pure spirit were not his only choices of appearance. There was also the physical manifestation of his spirit. In the beginning, he was beautiful and golden, but millennia of living in the darker realms had tarnished the still perfectly formed scales, blackened the delicate vanes of his feathers, and the once-vibrant color of his eyes had faded, becoming almost transparent. A gold-trimmed mirror, the only adornment in his chamber, reflected the degeneration that only separation from the Creator could cause. He fell to his knees.

"Oh, Father," he cried, "Why am I still so lost?" Banned from Heaven, unaccepted in Hell, he existed in a twilight of sorrow and remorse. And pride. His damnable pride . . . in his beauty, his mind, and his accomplishments. The mirror did not lie. His golden beauty was desecrated; his mind was so wretched that only the most tedious and meticulous work kept him from madness and total damnation, but his accomplishments! The books he loved had saved his mind and were the only source of pride left within him. He could not forsake them. Their value to celestial spirits, as well as their ability to instill within him the only sense of purpose he had left, earned him one earth hour out of every eight thousand and seventy so that he might remember the light and love that existed just beyond his reach.

Then he remembered he still had fifteen minutes left of that hour.

He stood up.

Looking beyond the walls of his inner chambers, he found her in her room preparing for bed. Not wanting to disturb her rest, he hurried so he would be at her door before she fell asleep.

Entering the dark room as Aidan, he retrieved the box with her belongings. *It was best*, he thought, *to get it over with now*. Another night of holding her and listening to the music of her heartbeat might cause him to lose his resolve completely.

He knocked on her door. When she opened it, he walked in with the box containing her work clothes, purse, and the other personal items she carried when she entered his bookstore. He could tell by her face that she instantly recognized the box.

He set it on her bed.

"Why did you bring me this?" she asked. "I haven't finished the book."

"I have decided that is immaterial. Since you find yourself missing the Earth world, I will take you to the portal. You have worked hard and have accomplished much. I am proud of your work. Come out as soon as you are properly dressed, and I will take you back."

She looked from the box to his face. His eyes, usually kind, amused, or annoyed, were merely empty. She smiled gently and tilted her head.

"Are you doing this because of what I said earlier?"

"What else would it be? You expressed a wish to return, so I am here to assist you."

She laughed softly. "Oh, Aidan, what I said earlier is that I look forward to being back in the world—"

"I know what you said, Helena. I was there. This is all my fault. I truthfully had no idea that remaking the book would take as long as it has, and it has wearied you. Therefore, I rescind your punishment. I will finish the book alone, and you can go back to your life."

"You understood what I was saying, but this is one of the few times when you didn't know what I was thinking. What I meant was that there is a kind of complacency in everyday routines, and I do miss that. Every day here is different. I never know what to expect, and many days are quite challenging, but Aidan, I wouldn't trade what I'm learning from you for anything that exists beyond the blue door." She pointed to the box. "So, please, return that to the storage room, and let's go on to the next step. I said I'd do this, and I will. It is fascinating to me. No more nostalgic remarks—I promise."

He nodded and picked up the box. Standing in the doorway, he paused, and she noticed that the expression in his eyes had softened.

"We'll make endpapers tomorrow," he said.

"If that is what comes next."

"It isn't what necessarily comes next, but it is, I think, the second most enjoyable step in the process." He looked down the hall, then turned back. "I'll, um, meet you in the garden . . . after you have rested." It really wasn't a question, but he wasn't leaving without her answer.

"Of course, Aidan."

He was halfway down the corridor when she called to him from the doorway. "Aidan?"

He stopped immediately but didn't look back. "Yes?"

"I'm curious. What is the *first* most enjoyable step in the process?"

"When you hold the finished book in your hand, of course."

"Of course," she said softly. "Good night, Aidan."

"Good night, Helena," he said, echoing the quiet tenderness of her voice.

Endpapers

Before joining her in the garden as Aidan, he went as spirit to see if she was there. If she was, he planned to return as Aidan, but when he saw her swimming, beautiful and sleek, his spirit slid into the pool and glided beside her. When she dove beneath the water, he followed, spiraling around her body like ivy on a tree. In the moments when she relaxed and let the current carry her, he drifted beneath her body, untangling the tendrils of her hair as they floated in the water.

Not trusting himself to watch her change into dry clothes, he left when she began to get out of the pool. If she were spirit, he would explore the intimacy she desired. If he were alive, he would have already loved her. Slipping back into Aidan's body, he straightened his clothes and freshened his appearance. Regardless of his efforts to find a middle ground, he could not see beyond this impasse, but there was time—there would always be time—and she was still with him.

***

I smiled when I saw him standing at the worktable.

"I thought you were going to meet me this morning," I said.

"I was, but I needed to set up the paper-making room to marble the endpapers, and it takes a while for the stabilizer to thicken the water. Perhaps I will have time later today."

"Well, you might want to check the thermostat for the pool first."

"Thermostat?"

"Yes, the temperature regulator."

"Why? Was there something wrong with the water?"

"It was unusually warm this morning."

"Did that bother you?"

"No, it was very relaxing, perfect for the evening, but I like it cooler in the mornings."

"I'll, um, check the . . . thermostat and investigate the problem at once."

"Thank you," I said. Curious, I picked up *Little Women* and lifted the front cover to study the endpapers. "Wait a minute. We're going to make these pages? You never said anything about making art."

"Helena, everything we've done so far has been art. This is just a more colorful way of expressing it. It is also a necessary step. Endpapers hide any stray threads and uneven corner folds, cover the raw edges of the leather, and add a bit of visual elegance to complement the elegance of the content. Although printing can be a journeyman's profession, I have never approached it that way. Craftsmen, for example, appreciate the perfection of the process and trust in the intelligence of their hands to achieve their vision. Artists appreciate the intelligence of the process and trust the perfection in their hands to achieve theirs. I find that making books is a combination of craftsman and artist—requiring bookbinders to trust both the perfection *and* intelligence of the process to achieve their vision."

"And trusting the intelligence or perfection of their hands?"

"You know as well as I that a computer does what we are doing in a fraction of the time—a very small fraction. The intelligence or perfection of the printer's hands, at least in your world, is the least important factor."

"True. But on this level," I pointed to the press and the objects on the table, "printers and bookbinders are craftsmen *and* artists?"

"Just as I said."

I nodded in agreement with—if not total acceptance of—his argument. Looking down at the endpapers again, I traced the pattern with my finger. "I've seen these pages in old books, but never thought much about them. They are very pretty."

"And somewhat difficult to match," he said. "Because of the multitude of variables, no two are alike . . . it's impossible."

"Even for you? I don't believe it," I said. Looking from the front endpapers to the back endpapers several times, I added confidently, "See? I knew it. These are perfectly the same." I held out the book to him.

"No, they aren't. There is one quite glaring difference."

"Show me."

"See this edge where the gold tips are lined with dark green?"

"Yes."

"Now look at the back endpapers; the gold tips are wider, and the dark green is narrower. You can barely see the darker line."

"But that is almost invisible."

"To you, perhaps. To me, it screams incompetence. I'm glad we have this chance to correct that error."

"But you just said it was impossible."

"It might yet be, but that is no reason we can't try," he said, pointing to the wide tray. "You will do some practice sheets until you feel comfortable with the process; then we'll see how close we can get to perfection."

I stuck my finger into the yellow-tinged liquid in the tray. "What *is* this?"

"It is water thickened with a kind of seaweed. Pick out whatever colors you wish to drop on the water's surface in any pattern you like."

"But won't it dissolve into the water?"

"No, I just said the water was thickened and stabilized. Trust me, the colors will lie on top; they won't sink even if you layer them."

"Okay," I said, picking up a small cup containing blue paint. "Well, here goes!" I poured a few dark drops on the water and watched them float and widen, thinning to a lighter shade.

Aidan pointed to the tray. "See how it works? Now, try a few more colors. Rather than pour, you can use these pipettes or the brushes to drop the colors on randomly, or you can make a pattern."

I looked back at the book and followed the designs with my finger. "That's very pretty, but how do you make the swirls and folds of the individual colors without turning it into the color of mud?"

"Carefully," he said, pulling a box from the shelf above the workbench. He set it down in front of me and opened it. Inside were several tools in different shapes and one black feather. I picked up the feather first.

"Eagle?"

"Um, no. An eagle feather is stronger and broader, and it is not much different than using this thin wooden dowel. This feather is from a, a black swan; it's far more delicate and rare," he said, taking it from me. "These items are all used to make designs in the paint. Since this one is for practice, we will use all of them at least once so you can see the effects each one can make."

The first tool I picked up was something that appeared to be a large comb with widely spaced wire teeth. When I looked closer at the tools, I saw several of these comb-like implements, each with teeth made of straight pins or nails, and some of them had two rows of teeth with staggered spacing. Inside the box, I also found a couple of short dowels of different diameters, a few paintbrushes, and at least a dozen small bunches of straws tied at one end, which I later learned were for scattering random paint drops of the same color by tapping them against my finger.

Aidan came over and stood next to me.

"Dip the comb into the water solution—a little deeper than the paint layer—don't submerge it too far or move it too fast, or we will have mud."

The comb glided through the solution, shaping the paint into points.

"Now," he said, "arc it and curve it around like a backward C."

I did as he instructed, and the points I had made became fan-shaped and beautiful.

"Oh, my God."

"Yes, um, it's a simple technique, but very effective. Each of these tools can be used to create a unique pattern without ever putting a paintbrush on paper.

To demonstrate, he picked up the feather, and with a deftness I did not expect, he made a perfect swirl of color in the middle half of the surface. Then, with hardly a breath between them, he changed hands and made the exact opposite swirl beneath it.

"I'm never going to be able to do anything like that once, let alone twice. Perhaps you should do this, and I'll watch."

"No. That is not our arrangement. But I will help. I will watch you, and when you have created something that you love, I will do the second one to match."

"You can do that?"

"I can try."

For three days, I did little else but make swirls, fans, arcs, figure 8s, and undulating waves on the painted surface. Every day, I got better as I concentrated on perfecting the effects I liked with the color combinations I loved. Aidan's patience was unending, and as I mastered one tool or technique, he would teach me another. For another three days, I learned paint layering and how metallic paint floats differently than non-metallic paint, and how best to blend them. When I suggested splattering some of the printer ink on the surface before adding the paint, he looked at me in surprise. He had, he said, never thought of doing that, and the gold gave a texture and shine to the practice samples that was unexpected and beautiful.

We used it in the final design. The endpapers were the only parts of the book we truly created together. We layered the paint on a double-sized tray so that the paint colors would match. On my half, I zig-zagged, swirled, and fanned the combed points into something I believed was elegant. Aidan matched my strokes exactly. He placed a double-wide sheet over the paint, waited a few moments, and then, lifting from the bottom, quickly pulled it out of the tray and laid it on a tilted board to drain. After a few quick corrections with the feather on the glistening paint, he took my hand and pulled me around to his side of the table.

The designs were exquisite. "Oh, Aidan," I said, clapping my hands together, "for the first time in my life, I feel like a real artist."

He smiled and said, "Helena, as I said earlier, you've been an artist since you printed the first page."

I laughed. "The *very* first page?"

He shook his head. "Well, maybe not the *very* first page." Looking at the endpapers again, he nodded. "So," he said, "you may be an Amy after all."

"Ah, no."

"Why, 'no'?"

"Because Amy was the only March girl who got everything she wanted."

"Well, you're still young, and I have heard that in the Earth world, anything can happen."

Before I could respond, he took my hand again. "I think this would be an excellent time for a celebratory swim," he said, leading the way.

We spent a longer time in the pool than usual, splashing like children and having a diving contest. Of course, there was no one else to judge, so we teased each other with scathing critiques. Finally, he looked at me. "Well, we can't put it off any longer. I'm sure the paint has set by now. Let's go see if we need to do it again."

We went to our separate privacy screens and changed into dry clothes, hanging the wet ones to dry. There was no embarrassment, no discussion; it was just what we did now.

Meeting at the door, we walked together into the paper-making room.

Standing in front of the paint-splattered table, I looked at the swirls of red and gold. My breath caught in my throat; it was one of the most beautiful paintings I had ever seen. My eyes flickered from one side to the other and found no flaws, but my opinion didn't matter. I didn't even ask if he thought it was perfect; I only asked, "Is it good enough?"

Aidan looked at the two halves for a long time. I knew he was scanning them a millimeter by millimeter—comparing them back and forth—looking for inconsistencies, irregular paint overlap, or the tiniest smear.

In complete silence, Aidan stared at the whirls, the points, and the blends, but the longer his eyes traveled from one side to the other, the more my mood shifted from elation to despair and back to elation. We had worked so hard to make this part of the book special, beautiful, and unique. I was almost shaking in anticipation when he finally turned and said, "It is good enough."

I twirled in happiness and went to hug him, but he stepped aside so quickly that I stumbled. He caught my arm to keep me from falling. I laughed at my clumsiness. "You don't dance, do you?" I asked, still smiling.

"Not for a long time," he said.

Binding

"Now that the endpapers are done—and beautifully so, I must add—we need to stitch the quires together and bevel the edges."

"Bevel the edges of what?"

"The pages, but we will get to that later. Right now, your task is to sew all the quires together as the first step in the binding process. So, are your hands clean?"

"Of course."

"Helena, there is no 'of course' answer to that question. We have gone through a great deal of effort to keep the pages pristine, and they must remain so. A smudge of any kind will result in disassembling the quire or quires, scraping and reprinting the damaged page or pages, then restitching."

"I'll be right back," I said, walking toward the sink. "Don't start without me!"

"Of course."

Aidan was cutting two lengths of thread when I returned and handed them to me with the candle and two needles. As I waxed the thread and threaded the needles, he held the endpapers for the front and back covers to the light to align them.

He put a pin into each corner to keep them from shifting, laid them on the table, and trimmed the edges.

"What are we going to do with those?"

"You are going to add them to the binding sequence."

"Aidan, I'm afraid to touch them."

"Your fear doesn't matter. Only the book matters. And, although it seems like part of the quire assembly, the correct insertion of the endpapers is critical to the binding. I've waited until now so that you would have the most experience in perforating and sewing the quires, so you should have no difficulty with these. However, because there are only two pages instead of six, you must use a deft touch with the stitching."

He layered a blank sheet on top of the front endpaper, folded it gently in half, and then did the same with the back. "You must punch these exactly the same so there will be no misalignment on the front and back covers."

I watched as he carefully inserted them into the cradle. Then he handed it to me with the awl. "You are only going through four pages, not six, so you don't have to press as hard."

Although he was talking in a normal—for him—tone of voice, I knew how much was at stake. Neither of us wanted to redo the endpapers; one, because they were perfectly done (or perfect enough), and two, I didn't think they could ever be more beautiful. Calmly, like I had done twenty times before, I double-checked the placement of the pages in the cradle, then I double-checked again. When I was absolutely sure, I picked up the awl and did not miss a beat as I punched the holes one after another.

I'm pretty sure Aidan held his breath until it was over. Without saying a word, I picked up a threaded needle and stitched each pair as I had learned to do.

I looked up as I handed the two sets to him and saw a smile that I never thought I'd see—a real smile—not only on his face but reflected in his eyes as well.

"Brava, Helena. You've done quite well so far. You've completed the printing and sewn all the quires *and* the endpapers extremely well. Now we are moving forward to a more, shall we say, dangerous part of the process."

"Dangerous? It's just a book."

"Helena, it's never 'just a book.' And that is beside the point right now. I only said it was dangerous in the warning definition."

"How so?"

"Because any errors or damage incurred during the binding can result in disassembly that can only be repaired by starting over."

"I, I don't want to do that."

"And neither do I, so pay close attention."

He set the box containing the quires on the table and removed the top package. He then took a roll of fabric out of his pocket. "This is bookbinder's linen tape," he said. "Three pieces must be sewn along the spine to connect the quires together. Do you see these three parallel sets of holes that are spaced slightly wider than the tape?"

"Yes, I do."

"The inevitability of smudges increases exponentially with the number of times you handle the book. When you sewed the quires individually, the pages were in the cradle, so they remained untouched. This time, to sew the binding tape to the pages, you will have to open and close each quire to insert the needles, which necessitates caution."

He cut three strips of tape about four inches long. Setting the back endpaper section in front of him, he then unwrapped the quire he took from the box and set it on top of the back endpaper assembly. He picked up the other threaded needle.

"You start at the bottom?"

"Yes. Every bookbinder does it a little differently. I weave the threads back and forth as I move upward. Therefore, not only am I attaching the binding tape and encasing it within the stitches, but I am also creating a netting over the spine. That way, most of the work is done on the outside of the book, thereby reducing the likelihood of damaging the pages. I will show you how to connect the first four quires. Here is a piece of paper. Make a note of the pattern and, most importantly, how the knots are tied and hidden at each end. If you get tangled, stop and call me. It's not hard, and you will be impressed by its strength when it is finished. Also, remember that tension is important—not too loose and not too tight."

"If I make a mistake?"

"I will carefully remove the threads so you can start over."

I sketched a diagram while watching him weave the pattern, and it dawned on me that he was essentially knitting with two sewing needles. My grandmother had taught me to knit when I was five. I don't do it much anymore, but some things you never forget.

"Are you ready to take over?"

"Yes, I'm pretty sure I understand."

"Pretty sure."

"Yes, Aidan, I understand."

"Thank you."

He walked to his desk behind the screen. Smiling, I picked up the needles and held the tension steady with my fingers as I added one quire after another, weaving the threads up, down, over, under, and through the pages, remembering to carefully knot and tuck the threads at every end.

I placed the front endpaper assembly on top and wove the needle through the last few pages. Tying the final knot, I called out, "I'm done."

"Done as in you quit or you're finished?" he said, walking over to the table.

"I'm finished," I said, turning the back of the book in his direction.

He picked up the scissors in one hand and the book in the other. Then, he slowly set the scissors down and, using both hands, carefully examined the book. He separated the pages, checked the interior stitching, and then turned it over, inspecting every knot, each twist of the thread.

"This," he said, "is quite wonderful. See where you anticipated the double twist here and loosened the thread? That was instinctual; otherwise, you would have had to back it out, and I cannot find a single place where you reversed any of the stitching. Impressive."

"Well, I . . .," I began.

"No. Don't tell me how you knew this. I can tell it wasn't the first time you ever worked with threads and a pattern. Just, for right now, let me enjoy this unexpected moment of appreciation for your work."

He flipped through the pages gently, looking for—I was certain—a smudge or accidental crease, but I knew there were none, and I watched as he shook his head and carried it back behind the screen where I could not see him.

***

In the same way he kept the fresh beauty of Helena's face a secret known only to himself; he would never tell her that the threadwork she had sewn that morning was as fine as anything he had ever done. Like sweets in a crystal box, he wanted to hoard those few memories to remember her when she was no longer there. They were the only pieces of her that belonged to him alone and were too precious to share.

Aidan knew that the cares and stresses of Earth life would bring back the shadows and anxiety to her face, destroying the serene loveliness that she had reclaimed while living with him. Equally destructive, and to his everlasting regret, he would soon apply a layer of paste over the perfectly woven threads on the spine of the book. Smiling grimly, he knew he would never see the beauty of her face or the exquisite artwork he held in his hand again, but neither would anyone else.

Such thoughts stirred up passions he could never express, and he decided he liked it better when he worked alone. Sighing, he removed a hammer from the bottom drawer of his desk.

***

I heard his desk drawer close and looked up. Setting a hammer and the book on the worktable, he opened several drawers in the small cabinet and took out a roll of thick cording, a two-inch wide strip of linen, and a paste pot.

"You were gone so long. Did you find anything wrong with the threads?"

"No. We can proceed to the next step. I just wanted a few extra moments to study the precise symmetry and simplicity of the netting. It was important to do that now because once it's covered with paste, I will never see it again."

"I guess no one will."

"No."

I looked at the array of tools and other items on the table. "This looks complicated," I said. "What are we doing next?"

"This," he said, picking up the scissors.

Seeing the scissors in his hand, I felt despair in the pit of my stomach, and my face burned with embarrassment because I suddenly realized it was all a joke. *He was just being sarcastic . . . he thinks my weaving is terrible*, I thought, watching the scissors in his hand. *He is going to rip out all the threads and make me do it again.* I waited for some scathing remark about how he was only kidding regarding my "precise symmetry" and that it was the worst mess he'd ever seen.

But it didn't happen that way.

With the scissors in one hand, he cut the cording into three two-inch pieces. Picking up one of the needles, he showed me how to sew the cord to the binding tape, catching the crossed threads with each stitch. I finished the other two. Then, with an apologetic look, he took the brush from the paste jar and covered my beautiful netting with a thick white paste, pressing it through the threads and between the edges of the quires, completely covering the spine of the book. When he had a thin, even coat of paste, he centered the scrim—a strip of loosely woven linen—over the spine. Then, using a thin, blunt piece of wood, he tucked the scrim smoothly over the spine and into the crevasses between the cording and the book, leaving an inch of overlap on both sides.

"I would have told you how to do that, but I knew I could do it faster than telling you, and the paste sets up quickly. Besides, you deserve a reward for your work this morning."

"It wasn't that big a deal—"

"Perhaps not, but let me think it was . . . okay?"

"If you wish," I said, mimicking his oft-repeated phrase.

He put the book between two blocks of wood and smiled. "You know what I wish, Helena? Since we cannot do anything else until the glue sets, let's take a 'dip in the pool,' as *you* like to say."

I got to my feet. "The last one in is a rotten egg!"

"That doesn't sound very pleasant, so I'd best hurry," he said, walking quickly toward the door.

I was faster, though, and beat him to the pool by two steps. "Ha!"

"So, tell me, what does a rotten egg do in this situation?"

"Anything the non-rotten egg asks him to do."

"And that would be?"

"Ummm," I said, looking around. "A backrub?"

"Do I do that inside the pool or outside the pool?"

"Haven't you ever given anyone a backrub before?"

"I have not."

"And you've never had one?"

"I regret to say that I have no experience with backrubs whatsoever."

She spread the towels in front of the pool and gestured to them. "Just lie down on your stomach, and I will demonstrate a backrub."

"If you wish."

***

He didn't want to lie on the floor. It was undignified, and he couldn't see her if he was face down. Still, she seemed to think this was a natural turn of events, and he grudgingly wished he had run a little faster.

When she casually sat on the small of his back, he almost came off the floor. He couldn't believe she wanted to be that close to him. The way parts of her body were touching his, he had not felt such warmth for centuries. It was several moments before he could manage to say, "Why are you sitting on me?"

"I can't give you a backrub if I can't reach your back. Am I hurting you?"

"No, I was just surprised."

"Well, cross your arms in front of you, put your head down on them as a pillow, and try to relax."

He didn't answer; he did as she instructed and willed himself not to move. Relaxing was not an option.

Before she lived here, it was only necessary to possess enough control of Aidan's body to move through the bookshop without stumbling. There was so little actual work that "looking" like he was busy was all he had to do. Therefore, he only needed to concentrate on moving his arms, hands, legs, and torso. He kept his facial muscles limited to smiling and other such minimal expressions as required by a shopkeeper. However, to keep up the pretense of "Aidan," he had pushed his sensory sensitivity into every nerve ending his spirit could reach. Maybe he couldn't dance or sing, but he could feel each of her fingertips as they dug into his shoulders and back muscles and feathered down his spine.

"You have nice shoulders," she said. "You must have been swimming for a while."

A muffled "Yes" was all he could manage with his head down.

Although he lay unmoving and silent, his mind rejoiced with every touch of her hands and knew that nothing for the remainder of his existence would bring so much pleasure. Just when he believed he could not stand it any longer, that willpower alone was keeping him from turning over and . . . *and what*? He could do nothing to please her.

At that moment, she hopped up and said, "Okay, Aidan, my turn."

He rolled over and stood up awkwardly as she settled down on the towel.

"Um, Helena, am I allowed to sit on you?"

"If you can do it without squishing me, sure."

"I think I can manage."

He placed his knees on either side of her hips and tried to remember the way her hands moved over his back so that he could replicate them.

"I will do this the best I can," he said, "but let me know right away if I hurt you."

"Don't worry, I will! Just start off gently and go from there. If you press too hard, I'll tell you."

"All right, then."

He smoothed the shirt over her back and felt the muscles and bone structure beneath it. Her neck was small, and he hadn't realized how delicate her shoulders were or how many tiny bones made up her spine. Aidan's hands were large, but they were soft, and he gently massaged her neck and shoulders. Then, with his fingertips, he rubbed the muscles on either side of her spine as far down as he dared. Working his way back up her back, he stroked the muscles over her ribs and drummed his fingers over the base of her neck, her shoulders, and the tops of her arms.

He sat back on his heels. He really didn't want to stop, but he couldn't think of anything else to do.

"Helena," he asked softly, "was that okay?"

There was no answer.

He bent over and looked into her face. She was asleep.

Smiling, he carried her to her room to rest.

Leaving Aidan on the hallway floor, he returned and lay down beside her. He knew she had secrets she would never share, desires he would never know, and although he had not seen them, he suspected that she had fires and passions of her own. Lying there, unable to touch her as spirit and forbidden to touch her as a man, everything he was wanted to devour her secrets and revel in her desires, but more, much more than that, he wanted to feed her fires until they consumed them both.

Only then could he be reborn—only then would he want to.

***

Taking a short swim after waking up, I found Aidan in the workroom—where, apparently, he lived when he wasn't in the pool or behind his desk—working on a vertical wooden press I did not recognize.

"Did you have a nice nap?" he asked. "I'm sorry my backrub expertise was lacking to the point you were bored."

I laughed. "No, I wasn't bored at all! That's the point; backrubs are supposed to relax you. And, you know, resting on the floor and listening to the water practically make falling asleep inevitable sometimes." I paused for a moment and continued, "I thought it was really quite nice, Aidan. Thank you."

"Well, if I'm ever a rotten egg again, I won't mind giving you another one. I could probably use the practice."

"Only if you let me give you one, too!"

"If—"

"Yes, I know, 'if I wish.'" I waited a moment, then asked in a softer voice, "What did you think of your first backrub? Did you like it?"

"Yes, I did. Though being my first one ever, I don't think I relaxed as much as I will next time. I really didn't know what to expect."

"Well, now that you do, we will definitely have to do it again." I put my hand on the press. "What is this used for?"

"Trimming the deckled edges from the pages."

"I like the pages like that! All uneven and soft."

He laughed for a moment. "Of course you do . . . it appeals to your artistic nature. The pages are trimmed because, one, it gives them a finished and polished appearance, and two, it is impossible to add the gold leaf unless they are even. So, to get started, I will place the book into the press, then you will trim the edges."

Picking up a smaller piece of wood, he showed me the blade. "Do not touch this. And, whatever you do, do not get your fingers in the way of the chisel edge while you are trimming. I promised to return you in the same condition in which you arrived, but I cannot do anything about missing pieces of your anatomy. Plus, on an equally disastrous note, any speck of blood will contaminate the entire book, and you will have to start over." He paused, then said, "And, before you ask, I will not do this for you."

"I wasn't going to ask."

"Um, hmm, perhaps."

Determined to do it myself—and do it perfectly—I watched carefully as he fitted the blade over the top of the press. He made one pass over the book, and I watched as thin slivers of paper fell from the press. He moved away from the worktable and walked to his desk behind the screen without looking back. I took a deep breath and thought about his hands on my back and wished I hadn't fallen asleep.

I put my left hand on the base of the book press to steady it and moved the blade up and down the length of the book. More shavings fell onto the table. Each pass of the beveled blade took another small bite as it moved inexorably from left to right, leaving a clean, straight edge in its wake.

He reset the book twice more so I could trim the top and bottom. When I finished, it looked like a brick of paper. That's when I learned why he had brought the hammer to the worktable.

"I will demonstrate shaping the spine," he said. "It takes a certain amount of pressure, and your shoulder and arm may be tired from the trimming."

"Okay, but I don't mind trying."

"No, I'll do it," he said. Holding the book down with one hand and the hammer in the other, he began pounding the spine, shaping the front and back quires into a slight curve.

"Why are you doing that?" I felt sorry for the beautiful book being literally pounded into shape.

"Rounding is important for a couple of reasons, all good for the longevity of the book. One, it keeps the book flat by preventing the unbound edges from splaying; two, it stiffens the spine, which, three, prevents the foredge from protruding. However, too much curve can cause the middle pages to collapse inward, meaning that each spine is curved a little differently based on thickness. Thinner books have a small curve or none at all."

As I observed this new (at least to me) technique, I slowly realized that Aidan had become lost in the process. I knew he no longer realized I was there as he measured the curve from side to side, checked the inner curve, and held the spine to the light, making sure it was straight, all the while treating the book as if it were fragile and priceless.

When he set the hammer aside and measured the curve for consistency from top to bottom for the fourth time, I said, "I think I'm beginning to understand you a little more."

"You are?"

"Yes, because I've been watching you so carefully."

"And what, exactly, do you think you understand?"

"I understand that these beautiful books that you love so much are like your children."

He put the book down on the table and took a step backward. "What do you know of my children?" His voice was demanding and almost angry, and his eyes looked dark and wounded.

Being alone with him had never scared me, but I knew I had somehow crossed a line and slowly backed off. "Well, nothing, of course, Aidan. I just meant that you put so much love and attention into each one of these volumes that they are like parts of you, you know, like children would be. I didn't mean anything else."

He looked at me as though he was trying to read my soul, and it took several moments before his face resumed its amiable expression. "Of course, that is an interesting observation. However, there are some things that are too personal, for many reasons, for us to discuss casually."

"Of course, I understand."

"Do you? Let's see. Do you have children?"

"Um, no."

"Why not? You are an adult female. You look healthy . . . and you told me you were married. Didn't you want children?"

"It's not that easy; bodies are complicated. Relationships are complicated."

"So, you do understand—a little—how such discussions can be difficult."

"Yes, I'm sorry."

"Be sorry for nothing; just do better."

I nodded and didn't say anything for the rest of the day. Neither did he.

He did not come to the pool that night, but the water was so warm and relaxing that, despite my earlier nap, I did not stay long but sought my bed early.

Edge Gilding

The book was back in the press when I walked into the scriptorium, and there were new items on the worktable: a narrow tin box, a cake knife, several small bottles next to a pipette, and square wads of fabric.

Within moments, Aidan entered carrying a board, a long, thin, flat brush, and a matching shorter brush with paper handles and two-inch flat bristles. He placed them on the table and started arranging the items in rows.

"Oh, goodness, Aidan, what is all this?"

"As I mentioned earlier, these are the necessary supplies for the edge gilding. You did notice that the edges of the book are edged in gold, didn't you?"

"Yes, of course, but I didn't know you did that, too."

The stunned look on his face was almost worth the sarcasm. But not quite.

"And who, Helena, did you think did it? You know by now that the pages are not printed that way." He paused in exasperation. "As I have told you, you are and, by all accounts, will be my one and only apprentice. So, yes, I do the gilt edging, so it is your job to watch and learn."

Still feeling the repercussions of yesterday's conversation and missing him during our pool time last evening as well as this morning, I could not keep my eyes from tearing up. "I won't apologize, Aidan; I will just try to do better."

He touched my chin and gently lifted it up until my eyes met his. "Please don't cry, Helena. I'm beginning to think that there is not a book in my library worth one of your tears," he said, smiling slightly. "It's just that some of your questions catch me off guard, and I react harshly. I promise to try to do better as well."

He moved his hand from my face to the book and sighed.

"Is there a problem with the book?"

He looked at me, no longer smiling. "The first answer to your question is 'no,' which leads to a much more resounding 'yes.'"

I looked from him to the book, then back at him, and nodded. "I see."

"What do you 'see,' Helena?"

"That you're afraid of the perfection slipping away."

"Yes," he said, breathing the word so it seemed to echo from somewhere deep inside him, and I felt the pain of the word as though it stabbed me in the heart. Without thinking, I sprang from my chair and wrapped my arms around him as much for myself as for him. I don't know how long I stood there, but it wasn't long. As soon as I realized he wasn't hugging me back. I stepped away.

"What was that for?" he asked.

"For courage."

"Thank you," was all he said.

He was still for a moment, then shook his head and smiled at me as though nothing had happened.

He wants a reset, was my first thought, but my next thought, *I guess we've had our first fight,* sounded ridiculous even in my own mind.

"Helena?"

"Yes?"

"Are you back from wherever you were wandering?"

I swallowed and, trying not to smile, looked up. "Yes. I'm here, watching and learning."

"Good. I'll start over." He took a deep breath. "Gilt edging is used for two purposes. First, it is a beautiful finish to the pages, but second—and more importantly—it seals the story and secrets of the text within the book, preventing the words from blending with the text contained in the other books in the room."

"So, each book is like a different broadcast channel?"

"Not an analogy of which I'm particularly fond, but in its most basic form, yes."

Looking once again at the array of tools and other unfamiliar items on the worktable, I asked, "How much gilt-edging am I going to be doing?"

He laughed to himself and tilted his head. "And what does an apprentice do?"

"She watches and learns, but sometimes, she gets to make art."

"I'll think about it," he said, walking over to the book press. "Now, for a little background. While you were resting, I put the book into the press, sanded the page edges, brushed on some sizing, let it dry, sanded it down, and then I did it again. The next step is to add a final layer of sizing and place the gold as flat as possible on the book's edges."

Opening the long, narrow box, he pulled out a piece of paper supporting a wide ribbon of gold leaf. Taking the long cake knife (or, as he explained, the "gilt knife"), he lifted the gold from the paper and placed it on the board ("gilder's block"). He trimmed it a bit and, taking the paper handle of the wide bristle brush, touched the bristles to the gold and lifted the entire ribbon in one piece. Tapping the bristles gently against the press released the gold leaf, and it settled perfectly over the edges. He blew softly to smooth any small wrinkles, then, taking the small square of linen, he dabbed and rubbed the gold leaf, gently pressing it onto the pages and picking up any excess moisture from the sizing. When that was finished, he took a piece of parchment paper, laid it on top of the gold leaf, and continued to press it onto the edges as he rubbed it with his fingers.

"Before I burnish it," he said, "I need to let it set for a few minutes. Do you have any questions I can answer while we wait?"

"How long?"

"Are you asking me how long it takes to do the entire process?"

"No. How long did it take you to learn it so well that you could do it perfectly without a misstep, tear, or fold?"

"Too long. I kept trying to find ways of doing it faster, um, more efficiently. What I didn't realize was that the process had evolved over hundreds of years with hundreds of little improvements by thousands of bookbinders until the process was as efficient as possible."

"You were trying to perfect perfection." Then, I remembered something my father once said. "My dad would say you were trying to reinvent the wheel."

"And he would be right. Once I realized my error, I worked within the process, and everything fell into place, literally! I did make some changes, such as pressing the gold in the correct widths and lengths, so it does not need to be cut or pieced. Which is good news for you because it means you don't have to scrape excess gold from the press before we move forward."

"Thank you."

The words hung in the air as Aidan picked up a long tool with a curved, almost hammer-like, end and started working it over the pages back and forth to polish the gold. I lost count of how many times he did this, but little by little, infinitesimal layers of gold were pressed and polished until only a gleaming and shining edge remained. When he took it out of the press, he slammed it against the worktable, releasing the pages, and I watched admiringly as he fanned the perfect gold edges.

As he tirelessly polished the gold, I thought of all the books in the room shining under the rainbow light. He had not only made those but perhaps countless others that were somehow "not perfect enough," and I developed an appreciation for the work he had done alone before I joined him in this big space.

"What do you do with the books that are not perfect enough? Do you have a room for them, too?"

"No, why would I keep them? I don't need to be surrounded by error-filled pages to be reminded of my own imperfections. I prefer rooms with volumes I can look at and enjoy."

"*Rooms*? I thought there was just the one room behind the shop."

"No. That is the seventh room. The other six were moved to chambers in the center of the spiral where the light is brightest."

There was a sudden tightness in my chest as I thought of all the books he had made in this soundless space. "How, how many books in each room?"

"Twelve hundred."

I was silent as I did the math, then gasped, "Aidan, that's more than seven thousand books!"

"Yes. And when the library behind the bookshop is full, I will move them to the center and begin again. Of course," he said apologetically, "there would have been more, but once I designed and built the press, I remade all the books I had printed and illustrated by hand." He gestured casually to the curving wall of books.

He said it so matter-of-factly that I accepted without further question that this was his life and the kind of man he was: creative, dedicated, committed, and yet, in my mind, so desperately alone.

Hours later, after the top edges shone as brilliantly as those on the side, he turned the book around in the press, looked at me, and said, "So, apprentice of mine who sometimes gets to make art, let's see how well you were paying attention." Then he stepped away from the worktable.

"What happens if I don't get it right?"

"Sanding off a poor application of the gold leaf takes about eight times longer than scraping a single page."

I picked up the sandpaper to prepare the edges for the first layer of sizing. "Then I guess I'd better not make any mistakes."

"It would be to your advantage."

I put the sandpaper down for a moment. "Aidan, wouldn't it have been more efficient to add the edging before hammering the curve into the spine? I mean, the gold would be so much easier to add to the edges if they were flat."

"Yes. On thin books, it is easier because there is no curve to the spine."

"What's the difference?"

"Helena, what happens to the edges when the spine is curved?"

I looked at the book in the press. "They shift inward."

He was silent.

"And tiny slivers of white would peek between the gold edges."

"Yes."

I picked up the sandpaper. "Will you stay?" I asked.

"If you wish."

I did not answer but went to work, copying every move Aidan had made, trying to be as methodical as he was. However, by the end of the application, I was afraid my hand would never be the same. I had gripped the handle of the burnisher so tightly my hand would not uncurl without pain. When Aidan said he would finish the burnishing because he wanted it to match the depth of color as the top and side edges, I absolutely let him.

Later, as we were in the pool celebrating the gilding being finished, he took my right hand and massaged it until it didn't hurt to straighten my fingers.

The Cover

"The outside of the book is to get your attention—the inside has to keep it."

"I can't believe you go through all this trouble for spirits who can never see the actual book."

"I don't, Helena. I 'go through all this trouble' because *I* can see it."

Once again, the supplies on the worktable seemed endless: a large rectangle of red leather, two very thin boards, the paste bottle, a knife resembling a scalpel, a small hand plane, a wide flat stick, and some pieces of scrap paper left over from my printing mistakes.

"And," he continued, "because I can see it, I will do the cover. If anything happens at this stage, we will have to begin again, and I am not sure either one of us has the patience for that." Then he smiled at me. "Unless, of course, you have an objection."

"Um, no, I don't really object," I said reluctantly.

"What's wrong? Was the cover something you were looking forward to doing on your own?"

"No, but I've come this far. I was hoping I could, somehow, finish it or, at least, help."

He was silent for a moment. "I see. Well, perhaps we can do it together. I will go slowly enough so you will learn, and then, when I've completed my part, you can burnish the gold lettering. You did an excellent job of that yesterday, and it is the last step before putting it on the display shelf."

"And then people in Heaven will be able to read it?"

"The *spirits* in Heaven who wish to will be able to conceptualize the characters, the setting, and the storyline."

"Okay. Is it all right if I put it on the display table?"

He laughed softly. "That will be difficult with your hands tied behind your back. You may watch from the doorway if it will give you a sense of accomplishment."

"Really? After all this time?"

"Why, yes. Nothing's changed."

"I'm still a vandal?"

"Yes. Just a more knowledgeable one."

I thought of every step, every page, every letter I had set, printed, reset, and reprinted, again and again. Aidan's punishment had fit my crime, and I suddenly knew how I would feel if, after all that care and work, someone had carelessly destroyed it.

"That's true," I said slowly, "on so many levels." I looked up at him. "You don't forgive easily, do you?"

"There are those who would say I don't forgive at all," he answered quietly, then smiled. "However, your unceasing and mostly uncomplaining diligence is beginning to convince me that I may have to make an exception in your case. Someday."

"I wish you would."

"Perhaps."

"Perhaps," I repeated. Then, taking a deep breath, I smiled back. "So, how do we make a cover?"

"Since all my books are the same length and width to fit the shelves, I have already cut the necessary wood for the covers. The depth, therefore, is the only variable that needs to be measured and, as you can see, I have already cut the leather. Before we start gluing the leather to the boards, I will place the boards on the top and bottom and confirm that the measurement is accurate."

Before measuring anything, however, he wrapped the pages in brown paper like a present, leaving only the spine free. "To make this process a little less dangerous, I wrap the printed pages to protect them from smudges, creases, and inadvertent drops of glue," he said as he fitted the boards to the front and back of the book. When he had them perfectly lined up, he placed the spine in the middle of the leather rectangle and brought the leather up over the covers until the ends met precisely in the middle of the book.

"Exactly right," he said to himself.

Flattening the leather on the table, he took the small plane and began shaving the edges of the front and back covers.

"Why are you doing that? You said the measurements were perfect."

"I'm not shortening the leather, merely thinning it so that the inside edges lie as flat as possible. It is necessary for them to be the width of a single piece of paper so there are no visible or tangible ridges under our endpapers."

When he finished shaving the edges, he looked at me and said, "I'll get another brush, and you can help with the pasting. It needs to be done quickly so it won't set up before the ends are perfectly matched on the boards." He paused. "And it has to be applied evenly, so no lumps."

"Right," I said, taking the brush from him, "no lumps."

I watched for a few moments, then began spreading the paste on the leather. Aidan folded it on itself and waited. After a few minutes, he unfolded it, scraped the glue off, and then together we covered it in paste again. As he put an even layer over the spine and linen scrim, I added more paste to the boards. When the pasting was finished, he repositioned the boards, fitted the leather, and secured the ends. Then, after taking special care to miter the leather so that it beveled perfectly when folded over the corners, he finished by pressing the leather over the cording on the spine with the flat stick.

I clapped my hands in appreciation, but he shook his head. "Too soon for that," he said, placing a blank sheet of paper between the wrapped pages and the covers. Sliding planks of wood on either side of the closed book, he slid the book into the press and moved it to the end of the table.

Having cleared a space on the table, he reached under the table and lifted what looked to me like a small hibachi grill onto the table.

"Steaks or chicken?"

"Excuse me?"

"That looks like the smallest outdoor grill I've ever seen."

"I guess it could be used for that, but here it's called a brazier, and it is used for heating the tools I need to polish the leather, as well as the letters necessary for embossing the title.

When I had run out of questions on how to use the polishing tools, Aidan walked over to the chest of typefaces and brought over a drawer of type I'd never seen.

"We have a few minutes, and since you know it so well, you could start pulling the letters we'll need for the title," he said.

I peered into the drawer. These were not the small elements of type that fitted into the composing slate; they were beautiful letters on six-inch irons nestled in their individual compartments. I lifted one and held it to the light. The letter was exquisitely formed: tall, impossibly thin, straight lines supported the flowing broad curves that seemed to begin out of air and disappear back again like delicately curled leaves entwining Greek columns. Looking more like jewelry than leather stamps, I was slightly breathless at their beauty.

"Aidan, did you make these?" I wondered out loud. "Or did you just dream them up, and they appeared?"

"I'm not sure what 'dream them up' means, so I will just answer your first question. Yes, I designed the typeface. And as earth metals are abundant in the fourth dimension if you know where to look, I constructed them from the resources available to me."

"By hand?"

"By hand and fire. How else would I do it?"

"A, um, die-cutting machine, I think they are called."

He nodded and smiled. "But I would still have to make the shapes, wouldn't I? And then each letter would need to be sanded and polished afterward. So, you see, my way was much more efficient."

"But it would have taken years."

"No, more. It actually took most of your lifetime, but what does that matter? They are exactly what I wanted and, if you will notice, very different from the typeface on the original book's ruined cover. Our book is the first one I've finished since I gave the letters their final polish, making you the first—and only— person to ever see them."

"I'm sure the cover will be beautiful," I said, carefully returning the letter stamp to its nest. This was not the work of a printer, but that of an artist in love with his work. I ran my fingers lightly over the other stamps, saying, mostly to myself, "So, all the time I was growing up, going to school, working, you were in here carving, sanding, polishing, and creating the most beautiful lettering I've ever seen, and, if I hadn't wandered into your shop, that chance would have slipped away. I don't know why, but the thought of losing that opportunity creates an ache somewhere in my heart? . . . mind? . . . that I would have felt forever had I known that such beauty existed within my reach, and I missed it."

"I didn't create the lettering for you."

"No, but the way you said it makes me feel like you did," I said, looking at him with new eyes. Then, I leaned over and kissed his cheek. "Thank you for that bit of joy, Aidan, whether you meant it or not."

I started walking toward the hallway and smiled back at him. "I've finished for the day."

"Where are you going?"

"I think I'm going to the garden, and—as you once said to me—'enjoy this unexpected moment of appreciation for your work.'"

I watched his jaw clench, and I knew he was forcing himself not to ask, so I added, "You can join me if you'd like. It's always nicer when you're there, but I might pick up my pillow on the way for a short nap."

"I will need to put these things away first."

"Of course," I said as I walked out of the workroom. Then, I stopped and turned. "And even though it may be tempting, please don't splash me if I fall asleep before you get there."

"I never do," he said.

***

Had he made the new typeface for her? How could he? He didn't even know she existed when he designed it. Yet, he instinctively removed this drawer when he intended all along to match the title lettering used on the original book.

No, he decided, he hadn't designed this typeface for her. She was just being romantic. Then, remembering the admiring look in her eyes, he decided to name the typeface after her. Not Helena, but her real name, Adrianna. He liked the feel of the syllables rolling around softly in his mouth as much then as he did when he read it on her driver's license. He looked forward to the idea of saying "I must go get Adrianna" and holding the delicate, curving pieces in his hands every time he finished another book. It would be a kind of reward to think—if only for a moment—that she was still in the room with him. Perhaps at some point, far into the future, he would stop calling the font by her name, and it would become just the "title font," but he knew it would never happen.

Or, he thought, he might design another typeface, *one more angular*. Not less elegant, just different, and set aside Adrianna's graceful curves and fine lines, but he knew he would not do that either and wondered abstractly how many millennia would pass before the name meant nothing to him.

He smiled, knowing it would be several, and put the items on the worktable away as slowly as possible—he had no intention of meeting her in the garden before she fell asleep.

***

I woke up in my room and felt a tinge of regret that I had no memory of being carried in his arms. Aidan hadn't joined me in the pool, and when I walked into the workroom, I understood why. All the items to complete the cover were set out on the table once again, but the brazier was now sitting on a ceramic platform next to the press.

He acknowledged my presence with a quick glance and nod as he turned and took the book out of the press. I reached over to help, but he held up one finger and said, "No. These tools are very hot; just watch."

Gently, almost lovingly, he laid the book flat, making slits at the top and bottom on either side of the spine, then folded the flaps inward. Taking two pieces of new paper cut to fit the open space between the spine and red edges of the leather, he glued one down to the inside of each of the cover boards. When the glue dried, he lightly sanded the inside of the covers.

After eliminating every speck of dust, he removed the waste sheets that had protected the endpapers from smudges. I held my breath as he tucked the edge of the waste paper into the spine, then, continually pressing, smoothed the endpaper over the inside cover from the spine to the edge. He worked steadily throughout the process without looking up once, and I knew that, once again, he had totally forgotten I was there.

He smoothed the endpaper several times as though trying to find a ridge, a bump, or a misaligned seam, but when he smiled, I knew there were none. Turning the endpaper over, he quickly glided a very thin layer of paste over the delicate surface. After resting the paste for a minute or two, he smoothed the painted paper over the cover for the last time, leaving an exact quarter inch of red leather binding showing around the edges of the beautifully marbled endpapers.

Then he turned the book over and did it again on the back cover, but before he glued the endpaper to the back cover, he went back and forth from the front to the back several times, making certain the endpapers were perfectly aligned. He propped the book open to dry as he cleared the table, leaving only the brazier and the heavy iron book press uncovered.

While the covers of the book were drying, he brought a pile of one-inch linen strips to the table and threaded two needles with some binding thread. Pulling a strip out of the pile, he folded it in the middle and kept folding it end over end until he had a fabric accordion about an inch square. Then, he took the needle and made an "x" with two stitches in the middle and knotted it to keep the fabric from unfolding.

"Can you do this?" he asked. "I need about a dozen."

"Of course. What are we making?"

"Fuel for the brazier."

"What? No charcoal briquettes?"

He reached under the table and pulled up a small bucket containing wood blocks cut into uniform pieces about two inches square. "I have these, but to burn smoothly and slowly, they must sit within a nest of the linen packets. Because the fabric is made of tightly woven natural cellulose fibers, it will catch fire quickly and burn slowly, igniting the wood without an accelerant, thereby creating an even heat."

"This seems like a never-ending process."

"I'm not in a hurry," he said. "But have no fear, Helena. It will end, and sooner than you might think." He laughed for a moment to himself. "Of course, I'm sure it seems that way to you. Never has one book taken so long to complete."

"Is that bad?"

"It makes it obvious that my apprentice experiment is a failure."

"So, you don't think you'll do it again?

"No."

I picked up a strip of linen and began folding it.

When he lit the brazier, I asked, "Do we need the heat for the book cover or just for the embossing?"

"Both, actually. Using tools to smooth the leather over the rounding and cording of the spine is important and gives a welcoming texture to the feel of the book, but it is also necessary to evenly distribute the adhesion of the different layers."

"The finesse."

"I like to think so."

Setting down the tenth linen packet, I picked up a shaving of the red leather from the table and rubbed it between my fingers.

"Why red, Aidan?"

"Not only red but this particular shade of red; not too vivid, not too dark, with a nice touch of blue—not so much to move the color into magenta and just enough to pull it away from the brighter cardinal shade."

"Do I want to know what kind of leather this is?"

"That is a strange question. I have no idea what you don't want to know. But to answer it—I think—it's goat leather, which is fine-grained, easy to dye, and, if the covers are not damaged, usually lasts a very long time."

"Never going to let that go, are you?"

"Of course not. It is the inescapable reason for our current situation."

"Is that so terrible?"

"No, but we have more interesting things to discuss."

"Such as, where are your goats?"

"My goats?" Then, for the second time, Aidan laughed out loud. Unlike the first time when I teased him about making earrings, this time his laughter, with its many voices and tones, rang through the rooms, resonating down the spiraling halls and back again. It was also contagious. I laughed with him until I thought my sides would burst, and still, the choir of his laughter continued.

It was several minutes before the echoing voices calmed, and he was able to look at me with eyes full of quiet mirth. "You keep doing that," he said.

"It was a fair question, but I'm not sure why it was funny to you. Though to hear you laugh, Aidan, is a wondrous experience."

"Is it? I'm happy you think so."

"The goats?"

"Not efficient or practical. Goats could live here, but as all flesh is static, they could not procreate, requiring a continuous supply of goats. Plus, I would need an abattoir within which to slaughter said goats, resulting in too much waste. What would I do with the rest of the goat after it was skinned? Therefore, I have no goats here."

I pointedly looked at the roll of red leather at the end of the worktable and realized that it was much larger than any one goat could possibly be. Then I understood. I looked at him. "You made that, too, didn't you?"

"I just needed one for the molecular analysis."

"I'm starting to believe that the fourth dimension is a slightly scary place."

"It can be. I think it all depends on your expectations. In my experience, it is the perfect place for a scriptorium."

"Only because that is what you made of it."

"Yes, but it was all that I wanted. It has been—and will always be—a gift to me."

"From God?"

"The Creator, who, according to a 19th-century hymn, created all things great and small, including, my dear Helena, the fourth dimension, as well as the fifth, the sixth, and the seventh."

"Oh."

"Yes. Um, perhaps we should discuss more relevant subjects, such as . . . ?"

But before I could suggest another topic, he added, "You've never asked what book I've been working on. You could, you know, ask that."

Grateful to move from speculating all that a fourth dimension could be, as well as the implications of three more, I asked, "All right, Aidan. What book are you working on?"

"*The Little Prince*. Have you read it?"

"Yes, one of my favorites," I said, then recited, "'It is only with the heart that one can see rightly; what is essential is invisible to the eye.'"

"You forgot the first part of that quotation."

"What is the first part?"

"'And now here is my secret, a very simple secret.'"

"And why is that important?"

"It is not necessarily important to the quotation, but it is important to me. These books are invisible to their intended reader until they want to be read. It is only through their heart's desire that they—the books—can be seen 'rightly.'"

"Where does the 'secret' become involved?"

"The spirits don't know who is making these books for them. They only know that the books are available for their pleasure in the great shared consciousness of Heaven. The secret, Helena, is that I am their anonymous translator, spending pieces of my eternity to give them stories, poetry, history, and science, and they will never know."

"Does it matter to you?"

"No. My efforts are not completely unknown," he smiled for a moment as though remembering something, then sighed, "or unappreciated."

He shook his head as though to rid himself of a thought and smiled again. "And that is my next book. Any recommendations for the one after that?"

"*A Tree Grows in Brooklyn*?"

"Done."

"*Jane Eyre*?"

"Also done. Do you only read novels?"

"Isn't *The Little Prince* a novel?"

"Yes, it is," he said, laughing. "Touché."

"Um, well, how do you usually decide?"

"Usually, I listen for requests. Sometimes, it's only a fleeting thought, a memory, a word or two of conversation—"

"Wait a minute. You can hear spirits' thoughts in Heaven? Who are you?"

"As I've said, I'm just me. In this four-dimensional space, or in the Earth-bound bookstore, I am Aidan, bookbinder and bookseller, at your service—and, as you know from our backrubs, there are no wings on me. Those are the physical spheres I am limited to, but my consciousness is occasionally allowed to travel even if it cannot reside—or even linger—in any other sphere. I thought you understood that."

"I think I understood some of that, especially the part about why you are here, but I thought you were alone. I didn't know you could converse with other spirits. I'm glad you have that interaction and can talk about books and things you've read."

Aidan stopped moving. I think, for a moment, he even stopped breathing because everything he was became silent and still. When he spoke, even his voice echoed that stillness and a sense of finality that almost broke my heart.

"I am a shadow to the spirits in the other realms. Even when I am permitted entry into their consciousness, I am like a chill wind, unwelcome, unseen, and unheard. A celestial spirit who rebuffs the glory of Heaven is always alone."

"Are there many of you?"

His eyes mirrored the heartbreak I felt for him. "No. Apparently, I am the only spirit who sought immortal humanity rather than Heaven. It is a rather limited existence when compared to Heaven, which is limitless. I guess you could say I wanted more, so I traded more for less, but it was my choice. Everything has its cost."

His smile brightened. "Which I have been happily paying for millennia. I believe I have, Helena, found my niche, as they say in marketing, and will spend whatever eternity I have making books for those gloriously happy spirits who wish to read them." He glanced over at the book drying on the table.

"And, speaking of which, I think it's time to return this one to the press."

***

He set the drawer of type stamps for the title lettering on the table a little louder than usual, then lifted his arms above his head and twisted from side to side.

"What's wrong?" she asked.

"It seems I have a stiffness in my shoulders this afternoon."

"Not surprising. You've been moving all these presses and equipment from the floor to the table for the past two days."

"We needed the extra room. Maybe I can work it out in the pool when we've finished. The book must rest until the glue is completely dry. Then we'll start a small fire. I'll do the tooling, and you can help with the gold embossing on the cover."

"Are we embossing the spine?"

"No, these books were created to remain flat—but never stacked and never to rest on their spine." He winced as he lifted the press to the table.

"Aidan, if you think it will help, we can delay the tooling and embossing, can't we? I can give you a back rub and work on your shoulders. If you relax a bit, it may make the rest go a little easier."

"You might have a point," he said, ducking his head so she wouldn't see him smile. "That is, if you don't mind. If I feel better, I promise to return the favor."

"Deal!" she said.

He had grown to like her sitting on his back while she kneaded the muscles of his shoulders and feathered her fingers down the sides of his spine. He reveled in the intimate warmth of her, and the joy of having her touch him, voluntarily and unafraid. He murmured the words he believed were appropriate to keep her there longer than he should have, but he knew she was waiting for her turn and ended the massage earlier than he would have liked. At her suggestion, he had taken off his shirt and was momentarily gratified with her frank approval of Aidan's body until he remembered it was Aidan's body that she admired.

He considered asking her to remove her shirt, but thought it was too much of an imposition considering his earlier stance, and was surprised that once she'd settled on the towel, she pulled her shirt over her head.

"Don't worry, I'll put it back on," she said, folding the shirt and making a pillow of it.

He looked at her lying there, her tousled hair, her gently curving spine crossed by a strip of linen holding a pair of his boxer shorts at her waist, and his socks pulled up to her knees. He had seen many women—all kinds of women in various stages of undress and in their most provocative poses vying for his attention—but nothing in his long existence matched how adorable or how desirable she was to him at that moment.

"Did you change your mind?"

"Um, no. I was wondering if I was too heavy when I rubbed your back last time."

She laughed. "No, it was perfect, remember? I even fell asleep."

"Yes," he said, pulling his shirt back on. "I remember."

Once again, with his knees on either side of her hips, he repeated everything he had done the first time while searching his memory for any additional information regarding massages. There was very little. So, he varied his technique, faster, slower, harder, softer, until he developed a kind of rhythm that appealed to him.

It had apparently appealed to her as well. He didn't have to look at her face to know she was asleep. Instead of taking her to her room, he picked her up and, gently covering her with her shirt, held her until she woke up.

His head was thrown back, and his eyes were closed when she stirred. Looking down at her, he watched as she wrenched herself from whatever dream she was having. When her eyelids fluttered and found his face, she smiled at him like he was the sun at dawn.

"Looks like I'm sleeping on you again," she said. "Sorry."

"No, I'm sorry," he laughed. "I must give the most boring backrubs known to man—or woman."

"No, they are perfect."

The way she was smiling at him made him want to kiss her more than anything in the universe, but there was nothing in the seven celestial realms that would entice him to kiss her mouth with Aidan's lips.

He stood and set her on her feet. "The last one in the pool is a rotten egg!" he said, diving in while she was busy getting back into her shirt.

Finishing

After a long swim and several minutes of playful splashing, I sat on the edge and watched Aidan swim laps. When he came up for air, I asked, "Does your shoulder feel better?"

"Yes, it does. Your technique is quite effective. Feels almost like brand new."

"Well then, Aidan, what would you have this rotten egg do?"

"Oh, Helena, that is a conversation for a different place and another time. I'll think about it and let you know."

"Well, don't wait too long. My teacher says we're nearly finished with our work."

"True, but I'll think about it anyway. It's an intriguing situation—having you once again in my debt."

Having abandoned all hope for his forgiveness, I said, "I know I said I was sorry for damaging your book, and I am, truly I am, because it means so much to you, but I am not sorry for one moment I've spent here, Aidan. Not one."

"That is very generous of you to say, given my limited hospitality and occasional lapse in manners. Thank you."

He started another lap as if I hadn't said anything of importance to him. On his way back, I tapped him on his shoulder.

"Yes?"

"Can I ask you a question?"

"Can I stop you?"

I laughed. "Probably not, but seriously. I was just wondering if you regretted bringing me here."

He looked at me steadily as though he were weighing different responses, then slipped out of the pool and sat beside me.

"I don't know how to answer that," he said finally. "I cannot say 'yes' because I have—for the most part—liked having you here. However, I cannot truly say 'no' because I am aware of how much I'll miss having you here. You have had, as you know, an effect on my life."

"Did you just say you will miss me?"

"I'm not sure. What I am saying is that I shall notice when you have gone."

"In what way?"

"It will be a lot quieter."

"Oh."

"And, of course, the work will progress much more efficiently."

"That's true."

"But I think it's going to take several more books before I stop listening for your footsteps or your voice and, um, answering most of your questions."

"So, you will miss me?"

"Only when I'm alone."

"But, Aidan, you are always alone."

"Yes." He paused for a moment. "However, I am looking forward to fewer disruptions, interruptions, and what you refer to as 'do-overs.' So, you see, every time I begin to miss you, I will simply remind myself of one of the reasons I do not miss you. It is my greatest wish that it will balance out."

"What if it doesn't balance out?"

"Then, while the thought of you lingers, I shall be either very happy or very sad. However, you are still here, so it is obvious I am willing to risk either outcome."

"Do you ever wonder if I will miss you?"

"No. Missing me will mean that you have nothing else in your life. With all that the Earth world has to offer, I do not know why you would miss me or this work. If you have learned anything here, take it and do with it what you will." He smiled and inclined his head. "With my compliments."

"You still haven't answered the question. Do you or don't you regret bringing me here?"

"You haven't been listening. I've just said plainly that I do."

"Oh," she said, her eyes misting over. "I'm sincerely sorry that I spilled tea on your book, Aidan."

His eyes were crystal clear when he looked at her and said, "As am I, Helena."

"Don't you want to know my real name?"

"It is immaterial to me. I am still 'Aidan,' so I expect you are still 'Helena,' and we shall carry on as we have begun. You could tell me, if you'd like, how you came to choose that particular name."

"It's my aunt's name. I always liked saying it; it sounded, well, just calm and feminine to me. Don't you like it?"

"Yes, but my opinion is irrelevant; I was just curious."

"Aren't you curious as to my real name?"

"No. I was far more curious about your motivations than your name."

"But you know, we're not finished yet. Perhaps you could teach me how to pronounce your real name; then, there would be no need for any pretense."

"I've considered it, but we have enough distractions from our work as it is. So, let us focus on finishing our tasks, shall we, Helena?"

"Yes, Aidan."

He reached over and handed me a towel as we moved to our separate dressing screens.

I didn't say anything, but every time he called me "Helena," he made my life with him seem even more unreal—almost as though we were actors in a play, with each word carefully scripted and every movement perfectly choreographed to keep us within our chosen roles. Every scene came back to me, and I watched the two cast members—Aidan, the teacher, and Helena, the student—

concentrate on hitting their marks and remembering their lines to accomplish the goal set forth in the first act. It didn't matter who the actors really were—that was just the unnecessary backstory for identities they would reclaim when the final curtain fell.

I tried to shrug off these feelings of inevitability while believing he was secretly looking forward to our last scene. I also tried not to mind. Even as my heart rejoiced that I was, in some small way, helping him restore something he so obviously cared about, my heart also ached with the acute awareness that each completed step brought us closer to the theatrical "fade to black" of our relationship.

***

It was late, and I was tired, but instead of going to my room, I walked along the curve of the wall of books, scanning titles as I quickly moved past section after section of books. At first, the books were published in English, then Dutch, French, German, and Italian. A multitude of Russian volumes came next, then Asian languages, Greek, and Latin, and many were not in any language I recognized. I didn't stop until I found them. Bound not with red hard covers, but soft white leather, I pulled one of the delicate volumes slowly off the shelf. Looking around and not seeing Aidan anywhere, I sat on the floor and placed the book carefully in my lap. I took a deep breath and opened it carefully. There were no endpapers because they were not needed. Handprinted in a language I could not understand, each letter was formed as perfectly as though it had been printed by a machine. But no machine type could impress the power and beauty I saw on that single page or duplicate the delicate nuance of the calligraphy, its thin lines, and the elegance of the perfectly shaded curves that I recognized instantly.

As if the words were not wondrous enough, an illustration at the beginning of each chapter took up almost a quarter of the page.

Colorful, gold-tipped, exquisite drawings of animals and graphic elements surrounded, supported, and enhanced the first letter of the first word. Examining the intricate details, I felt myself falling into the page—my breathing became gasps. Without warning, the admiration and reverence that filled my mind with awe cascaded into my heart with the sudden awareness of an underlying passion, love, and longing controlled by a hand that didn't falter. I knew that kind of self-discipline came at the price of great pain. My eyes burned as exultation turned to pity, then compassion. I caught the tears with my sleeve before they dropped on the perfect page, then buried my face in my hands.

I felt the book being taken from my lap and heard a soft sigh as it was returned to the shelf. A moment later, Aidan lifted me from the floor.

"I, I washed my hands," I managed to say between sobs.

"I know you did," he whispered.

He carried me to my bedroom and tucked me in as though I were a young child. He did not leave me but placed the chair near the bed and silently held my hand until I fell asleep.

When I went back the next morning, all the books with the white covers were gone. Standing in front of the empty shelves, I said, "Aidan?"

"In the workroom," he answered.

I walked quickly toward the sound of his voice.

"You moved the handwritten books."

"I know."

"Why?"

"You saw beyond what I created them to be. Forgive me for wanting to capture forever a moment I can never have again."

"I don't understand."

"If I had left them on the shelves, you might open another one out of curiosity or to admire it, but you will never again feel the rush of emotions you felt when you saw the pages for the first time."

"For the books or your artistry?"

"How you feel about me is irrelevant—only the books matter."

I smiled understandingly. "They were beautiful, Aidan."

"All of my books are beautiful, Helena."

"Yes," I said, "they are."

I looked down at the book we had nearly completed and thought of the books I would never see again. My eyes filled with tears, but I blinked them back.

"I will remember that moment forever, too."

***

Without another word, Aidan started a small fire in the brazier. He first made a nest of the linen squares, then, placing a handful of wood cubes in the center, covered them with the remaining squares. He took two medium-sized rocks and, striking them together, created a spark that the linen caught immediately.

When the wood began to glow, he placed a metal plate over the side of the grill and positioned two large hammer-like instruments on it. Pulling the drawer with the title letters closer to the heat source, he began removing the beautifully shaped letter stamps for the cover, setting them alongside the edge of the grill. While they were heating, he went into the paper-making room and brought out a large scrap of linen that he had folded into several layers. When he set it on the table, I touched it and noticed it was wet.

Before I could ask, he said, "For regulating the temperature of the roller. Sometimes, they heat too long, and the damp cloth cools them down. I also need it to keep the leather damp."

"Can I help with this?"

"Are you suggesting I let you near an open flame?"

"Yes, of course."

He laughed softly to himself and said, "No. I remember—too clearly—the last time I let you near a heat source, so, once again, you can sit there and watch as an attentive apprentice should without running the risk of burning her fingers—or anything else—again."

Duly cautioned, I sat quietly as an "attentive apprentice should," as he ran the damp cloth over the leather. Lifting the heated iron, he lightly rolled it over the cover, especially around the indentations and cording on the spine. At first, I didn't think it made much of a difference, but when angled to the light, I could see that the leather was smooth and inseparable from the book.

Setting those tools aside to cool, he picked up each of the title lettering stamps and set them around the brazier like a sunburst.

"Usually, planning the cover lettering takes longer, getting the spacing top and bottom and side to side correct the first time is crucial," he said, "but since I've already done this, it will take considerably less time even though we are using a different type. The only thing I ask is that you not distract me in any way. We've come this far without a major incident; let us finish that way as well."

Somewhere within me, a rebellious imp wanted to wait until a critical moment, then suddenly cough very loudly, but I pushed her back to a quiet place because the last thing I ever wanted to be was responsible for seeing that look of heartbreak on Aidan's face again.

Oblivious to my inner struggle, he opened a drawer and removed a three-inch square pad of paper. As I watched, he carefully pulled back the first page, and I saw a four-by-four-inch square of gold leaf. Lightly brushing some of the cellulose mixture over the front of the book, he then used the gilt knife to lift the gold leaf and center it on the front cover.

The stamps were sharp. The lines were thin and crisp, and the curves flowed around them like delicate wisps of golden smoke. When he finished embossing the title, he sat back and looked at me.

"Well, Miss First-and-Only Apprentice, what do you think?"

The letters were just as graceful and exquisitely formed as I had imagined them. I didn't want to answer too quickly, but as my eyes traveled over the script, I was suddenly struck by how much the elegance of the lettering resembled the beautiful swirls of the endpapers.

"The cover is every bit as magnificent as I thought it would be, Aidan. Remember how you felt about my weaving on the spine?"

"I'm not likely to soon forget it."

"Well, multiply that by ten—exponentially—and you'll have a small idea of how I feel about the beauty and perfect symmetry of these letters."

"That much?"

"Yes."

"Well, it's going to look even better when you burnish the letters."

"When do I do that?"

"Are your hands clean?"

"I'll be right back."

"Yes."

When I returned, I found the book on the table in front of my chair with a brush with long bristles to the right.

Under the book was a large piece of paper I instantly recognized as one of the sheets I had printed and scraped. I flashed back to those few days at the beginning . . . they seemed so long ago.

"Helena."

"What? Yes, I'm sorry. I saw the wastepaper and had a moment of nostalgia for those early printing days."

"Well, then, you know what it's for."

"To catch any of the gold that is brushed off the cover."

"Yes."

I picked up the brush and looked at him. "Softly and in circles?"

"Excellent deduction."

"Sarcasm?"

"No," he said, looking surprised. "Pride."

"Oh, well, thank you."

I took the brush in my hand and began making slow circles over the cover. The bristles were stiffer than I thought they would be, but I knew Aidan wouldn't have, at this point, sabotaged his own creation by giving me something that would scratch up the cover. However, the bristles didn't scratch the finish at all, but the burnishing took longer than I thought it would, as each pass removed only a slight amount of gold.

When about ninety-nine percent of the excess gold was removed and neatly deposited on the wastepaper, he took the book from me and, with a small stick with some cotton twirled at the end, lifted off the remaining specks. Pulling a clump of frayed linen threads from his pocket, he polished the gold lettering to a shine.

"Only one last thing to do," he said as he carefully removed the brown wrapping paper.

Its glittering pages unfurled, he turned the book around so I could see it. It looked exactly like what it was: a golden box of secrets, stories, dreams, and, above all these things, a book fit for angels.

"And now?" he said.

"It is stunning . . . and unforgettable. Thank you for letting me see it and letting me be a part of its creation."

"You're welcome. Are your hands still clean?"

"Yes."

"Then, here," he said, putting our book in my hands. The leather was still warm and, just like the first one, felt as though it was made just for me.

Aidan was right. Holding the finished book *was* the most enjoyable part of making it.

Closing Time

He took the book from my hands and set it aside.

"Helena, I am sincerely proud to announce that your apprenticeship has come to a successful end. If you don't have any further questions, I'll bring the box holding your things to your room so you can get dressed and return to the Earth world."

"Now?"

"Yes, aren't you ready to go home?"

No, I'm not ready to go home, I thought, with my heart beating so fast I was afraid he would hear it. *I need more time.*

"Aidan, I'm not sure . . . I think I need to sort through some things—find a way to put this experience into some kind of workable context—before I leave. Besides, aren't we going to have our celebratory pool time first? And then, perhaps I can rest. I'm not sure I can adjust so quickly from this environment to Earth time without a little mental and physical preparation."

"You knew we were almost finished. Why haven't you prepared—at least mentally—to return?"

"I have, a little," I said, "I just didn't expect it would be so abrupt. Can I have another day to get used to it?"

"As you—"

"Wish?" I answered.

"Yes. I'll put this book in my library and meet you at the pool."

"Last one in—"

He interrupted me. "No rotten eggs this time, Helena. Besides, you still owe me."

"True. Okay, one backrub when you get there."

He nodded and, carrying the book with him, left the room. I watched him leave, the rhythm of his stride, the set of his head, and I knew I would miss him every day for the rest of my life. I had never spent so much time with a man, any man. Even when I was married, I worked, he worked, he was on the computer, I was in the garden . . . no, not then, not even when I was a child, had my father watched over me with such care.

I was spreading out the towel for Aidan's backrub when he arrived.

He shook his head. "That's not what I want from you, Helena," he said.

I didn't know what he meant by that, but I didn't give up easily. "That's okay, we can trade backrubs, and then I'll still owe you, you know, whatever."

"All right, but you first, so you won't fall asleep on me—or under me, as it were."

"Okay," I said, making myself comfortable on the towel. I thought about taking off my shirt, but decided to leave it on this time. There was nothing in his manner that indicated it was something that remotely interested him.

***

Aidan was grateful for the shirt between his hands and her skin. He didn't want her to go back to the Earth world, but he could not make her stay. She did not belong to him, nor did it seem that she wished to. Therefore, he knew exactly what he wanted from her: a way to make it easy for both of them when the time came for her to leave.

Rather than caresses disguised as massage strokes, light feathering down her spine, or fingertips etching invisible wings across her shoulders, his strokes this time were methodical, firm, and brief.

"That didn't take long," she said.

"I didn't want you to fall asleep before you reciprocated."

"I wouldn't do that."

"Um, hmm, recent history would indicate otherwise," he said, smiling down at her. Bending over, he helped her up. "Do you mind if I remove my shirt?"

"No, not at all."

"Thank you."

It was foolish, he thought, trying to prolong this particular pleasure when his mind was so overwhelmed with thoughts of her body to even feel the touch of her hands on his back, but he knew she was leaving, and eternity was a long time.

Too soon, she stood up and, laughing, jumped into the deep end of the pool. He got up slowly and put his shirt on to join her.

An hour later, he knocked on her door.

She opened it. Her hair was still damp, and there was a drowsiness at the edges of her eyes that he knew meant she needed to rest.

"I just wanted to bring your things," he said, setting the box on the chair near the table. "I know tomorrow is going to be an adjustment for both of us, so get as much sleep as you need."

She walked over to him and placed her hand on his chest. "Thank you for everything, Aidan."

"Of course. We had an arrangement, a 'deal' as you like to say. I think we both fulfilled our parts quite well."

"Yes. Yes, I believe we did," she said without removing her hand. "Aidan, can I ask you something?"

"Yes, you can always ask, although I must always have the option of not answering."

"Of course," she said, pausing as though she had forgotten what she wanted to say.

"Helena?"

She took a deep breath. "Aidan, since this is the last night I'll spend in this room, I was . . . wondering if you . . . might like to share it with me. Stay with me, I mean."

He shook his head and opened his mouth to speak.

"No, not for that," she said, interrupting him. "Just to have you close to me."

Aidan kept his face expressionless, but his voice was gentle. "I regret, Helena, that I cannot do as you ask. First, I do not think it is fair to you to pretend a relationship that does not exist, and second, if I do as you ask, I'm afraid that delicate balance between whether I miss you or do not miss you will be irreparably shattered."

She nodded. "I understand. For me, too, I guess. I'm sorry, I didn't think about how it might be for you."

"In fact," he added, "that was my rotten egg request. It would be easiest for both of us if you left whatever feelings you have for me, or our time together, here when you leave. So, when you take your things from the box, put your feelings and memories in there and close it up. I promise to guard it as faithfully as I have everything else that belongs to you."

"And I'll always know that those feelings and memories will be with you?"

"Yes."

"I can do that," she said, her voice breaking. She ducked her head for a moment and, taking another deep breath, smiled brightly up at him. "I will do that, Aidan."

She rose up on her toes and gave him a quick kiss on the cheek.

"Thank you," she said.

"No, darling Helena, thank you."

Without another word, he turned and swiftly left the room.

His mind raced in a dozen different directions as he returned to his chambers. He wanted to stay with her. He shouldn't go back to her. She had invited him. He should just let her go. Why couldn't he go back to her? He'd gone before without her permission. He remembered the nights when her dreams aroused her, when she even whispered his name, and he could have so easily granted her subconscious desire. He had to force himself to leave her because even when her mind called out to his, he could not answer her. Perhaps he still couldn't be himself that night, but she wanted him next to her in the darkness of her room. She might touch him inadvertently. He might reciprocate. Why not let Aidan spend the night in her bed? Aidan had hands that could touch her, a mouth that could taste her, and a body that she wanted. By the time he reached his rooms, he knew that he could not refuse her. Especially when a night with her, acknowledged and embraced, was something he would have killed to claim.

He decided it didn't have to be a big entrance. A single light tap on the door, just loud enough to wake her. Then he could quietly slip into her room . . . her bed . . . her arms. He could hold and caress her as the man she desired. In his mind, he saw her smile, adjust the cover, and move her head slightly over on the pillow for him. It would be so easy to leave Aidan's body as she slept and have her as his own. All the reasons that had kept him from her suddenly didn't matter. She had asked him—he had not entrapped or seduced her—there was nothing in the rules to stop him now. He had her permission and was free to do as he pleased.

And he knew she would please him for the nights were as long as he wished to make them.

He paused at her door and raised his hand to tap it—then stopped. He could hear her voice through the door. What was she saying? It sounded like she was reading her book aloud. Perhaps she was rehearsing something she wanted to say to him. Maybe she was angry at his refusal, or maybe she was just lonely and talking to herself. Not knowing what he was walking into and unwilling to disturb her in case she'd changed her mind about wanting him, he left Aidan's body in the curve of the hallway and slipped through the wall unseen.

Sitting up in the bed, her head bowed, and her hands clasped in front of her, he heard her say, "And dear God, please bless Aidan, for all his patience and hard work, and don't let him feel too alone when I'm gone. With a grateful heart, I pray. Amen."

He was stunned.

Adrianna, his beautiful, perfect Adrianna, was praying. In this dark and desolate place. For him.

He moved away from the wall and quietly surrounded her. The tears caught between her eyelashes disappeared as she settled into her pillow, and the raggedness of her breathing smoothed and slowed. Although she could not hear him, he talked to her while she slept about how wonderful she was and all the ways he would miss her presence in the loneliest sphere of the universe.

The Dénouement

We walked into the bookshop together. I glanced at the clock; it read 12:45, exactly as when I had left.

Smiling, Aidan stepped forward. "Goodbye, Helena. You've done excellent work."

"It's not Helena, Aidan."

"I know," he said, reaching to touch my hair for a moment, then, suddenly, he pulled his hand back as though he had touched something that did not belong to him.

"Aidan, I was your apprentice for quite a while. Do you think I've changed at all?" I said, twisting around. "I know you said I wouldn't change, but I don't have any way of knowing, so before I step back into the world, I just wanted to ask if I look the same to you."

I would like to say that he merely glanced at me, but he scrutinized my body, from the hair he would not touch to the scuffed shoes on my feet, as though cataloging and comparing every inch of me.

"The only physical difference that I can ascertain, Helena, is that you look less anxious than when you arrived. Whether your accomplishments have granted you any wisdom, I may never know."

"Thank you," I said, watching him walk toward the front door, but before he had time to slide the key into the lock, my eyes wandered to the tea and coffee display.

"One other thing, Aidan, if I may. Is there any chance I could have another tea to go, please? It was so delicious, and I'm still a customer."

"Of course." He slipped the key back into his pocket and walked over to the pristine array of teas, coffees, and biscotti in the crystal jar. He made the tea exactly as he did before, then poured it into a cup and pressed the lid on tight so that it would not spill.

"Here," he said, handing me the tea. "A souvenir of your apprenticeship to help you remember to treat all books like the precious things they are."

Breathing in the tea's unforgettable fragrance, I looked down at the cup and back at him.

"So, what are you going to do now? Wait for another clumsy person to walk in and teach him or her how to make books? It seems like a heck of a way to spend eternity."

"The door is unlocked for one hour, one day a year, if I have books to sell." He glanced up at the clock. "And I have only eight minutes remaining for this year. You get to go back to your life with a story that hopefully no one will believe, and I will return to my scriptorium to make more beautiful books. Next year, I will unlock the door somewhere else, and perhaps, just perhaps, someone as lovely as you—but decidedly more attentive to signs—will walk into my bookstore."

"How lucky for them," I murmured, dreading my next few words. "Aidan, am I banned forever?"

"Yes, but you knew that before you asked, didn't you?"

I nodded. "How long was I here? In Earth time, I mean."

Without hesitation, he said, "Ten months, three weeks, and two days—almost to the hour."

I laughed a little. "I guess I was a slow learner."

"Yes, but you learned. That's what makes all of this beauty worthwhile," he said, pointing to the books in the backroom. "Knowledge is its own reward."

I smiled and nodded. "I guess I should thank you for that, too."

"Ah, no," he said, "thank you." He didn't move but stood looking at me for a moment. "And, you know, you worked so hard, and, speaking of souvenirs, I promised you a gift. So, here. I made this for you."

***

Aidan slipped his hand into his pocket, and when he opened it, a small ring made of two gold wires, one wrapped around the other like ivy on the trunk of a tree, rested in the center of his palm. Three small designs were engraved on the spaces between the coils.

"See these markings?" he asked. "This one is for the sun, this one for the moon, and the last is for stars." He waited, but she didn't say anything. "If you don't like it, it's okay. I don't mean anything by it, of course; working on it just gave me something to do while you rested. You—"

"Aidan, please stop talking."

She lifted the ring, looked at the designs, and smiled. "I've never seen anything lovelier," she said softly, "but you know I cannot accept it."

"You don't have to wear it, you know, as a ring. I'm not asking you for anything, not for a promise or any kind of commitment. That would be impossible. A ring was the only thing I thought I could make out of the gold that you might like . . . I'm quite sure earrings are beyond my expertise."

She shook her head slowly and smiled up at him. "No, it would be pretending a relationship that cannot exist. Just as you said last night." Lifting the ring from his hand and sliding it onto his smallest finger, she said, "You wear it . . . to remember me by."

"If you—"

"Yes, Aidan, I do wish—so many things."

Simultaneously, they looked at the clock; the seconds were counting down. Without another word, he moved towards the entryway, and she walked to the back of the store to take one last look at the beautiful book they had made for Heaven's library.

He stopped at the front door and took the key out of his pocket. She stopped at the door next to a large sign that read "Do Not Enter."

"I'm sorry, Aidan, I can't do it," she said, opening the door a bit wider.

"Do what?"

"Let it go."

"The ring?"

"No. You."

She turned and, looking into his eyes, popped the lid from the cup. With a single, graceful movement of her hand, the contents of the cup swirled and cascaded over the perfect books, dripping from shelf to shelf and puddling on the polished display shelves nearest the floor. Laughing joyously, she turned and smiled at him like a young girl who had won a prize.

"To remaking paradise!" she said.

The clock chimed one. The key in Aidan's hand fell to the floor. He turned and looked at her. "Well, my dear, it would seem that the question as to whether you have gained any wisdom has been definitively answered."

"What do you mean?" she asked, still smiling.

"Do you know what you've done?" he asked evenly. He did not smile back but walked toward her slowly and deliberately, almost as though the clock didn't matter any longer and he had all the time in the world.

"Yes, I do. I'm going to stay here with you for another year and help you remake the books in the room, and then I'll go back to work."

"And that isolation with me is all right with you?" He stopped in front of her, blocking her view of the shop.

"Of course! Or I wouldn't have done it." She placed her hand on his chest. "Oh, Aidan, I just don't want you to be alone."

"When did you decide to do this?"

"This morning. I tried to gather my feelings and close them up in the box like I said I would, but I couldn't leave them, Aidan. I just couldn't. So, I thought if I damaged some more books, you would make me stay. You know, like you did the first time."

"You could have just asked."

"I was afraid you would say 'No' because I was banned."

Delight and dismay fought for control of his mind. He never thought her capable of such a grand gesture to keep him from being "alone." Oh, the preciousness of her statement! Solitude was the very reason he created the scriptorium. But now it was going to be different, so unexpectedly different, that he laughed softly to himself. Covering her hand with his, he said, "I would have said anything to make you stay, but it had to be your decision. That free will thing, you know."

"Then everything worked out."

It would take a long time, he thought, *to replace all the books she'd destroyed*. A very long time, and what made it all so perfect was that he was blameless. A rare circumstance, indeed. Her innocence and free will had absolved them both. This time, he laughed aloud.

"Why, yes. Yes, it did."

***

He softly touched my hair and my shoulders. *Yes*, I thought, *he's going to kiss me*. Then his hand circled around to the back of my neck. I felt my knees get weak, and I wanted him to hold me. I tilted my head back and closed my eyes. There was a faint clicking sound in the silent room, and I could sense the brightness around me begin to recede. I tasted a whisper of smoke. His fingers tightened at the base of my neck.

"Now, because you want it so badly, you will stay with me, Adrianna. Yes, I know your name—I've always known your name, and before too long, you will know mine. All of them."

At the sound of my name, I opened my eyes, and the man I had known only as Aidan was gone. Holding my neck so tightly I could barely move was a man-like creature more terrifyingly beautiful than Aidan could ever be. Taller and broader, his skin was the color of embers, and his eyes burned like living flame. Yes, I knew his name. Caught in a trap set by the father of lies, words stuck in my throat. In desperation, I looked past him and watched the front door slowly disappear.

"No . . . finesse . . . ."

He laughed again. "Probably not, but give it time, Adrianna, we have eons to get it right. And, you know, it wasn't that long ago when women were simpler; all I needed then was an apple."

"Is, is Aidan dead?"

"Aidan has always been dead. About eight years now. He's my favorite mask—trustworthy, affable—the perfect salesman."

"Where is he?"

"In the dark room of your nightmares."

"Am I dead?"

"No, but where we are going, your body will, shall we say, only get in the way."

My skin felt hot. I looked down. My flesh had become iridescent scales of pale gold, and when I saw the ring on my finger, I knew there was no going back.

"Where's, where's my body? My clothes?"

"With Aidan and the others, of course," he said with a grin. "However, unlike the others, your body is warm and waiting for you."

"For how long?"

"For as long as it takes to make a book."

"*A* book?"

"Yes. For as long as it takes to make a book eight hundred and seventy times. That is how many books were in the library you ravaged. So, at your, um, shall we call it, 'production rate,' about eight hundred and seventy Earth years."

"Oh, my God."

"Too late for that, my dear, far too late."

His eyes moved slowly from my head to my toes and back to my face. "I wouldn't worry too much about it, though. We have plenty of time for—what did you say? 'Remaking paradise'? Of course, it may not be exactly the paradise you imagined, or it may be more than you ever thought possible. I mean, just look at you now . . . so fresh, so alluring . . . I think I may be your 'someone' after all."

Darkness continued to descend as his exultant laughter echoed throughout the rooms.

The red covers of the books began to burn.

Speechless, I could only stare through the smoke and the fire into his face as his eyes flashed and shone deeply into mine.

**

No longer having a reason to rein them in, his passions rose to the surface. Nothing could keep them apart now that she had deliberately, freely, and blissfully chosen to be with him. He did not care that horror had chased the beauty from her face and fear clouded the intellect of her mind. He knew that unspoken desires smoldered within her, and now all he wanted was to search them out, ignite them, and luxuriate in the blaze of joining his inferno to hers. With that thought, he decided it would hardly be fair to resume their work on such a day when he had so many other creative amusements—far more interesting than bookbinding—that he wanted to share with her.

He pulled her close. The warmth of her body awakened centuries of suppressed longing, but the memory of his whispered confession in the deep purple of her room gentled the maniacal laughter. *There was time,* he thought, and she was still with him. He looked at her, and his voice became almost tender.

"To remaking paradise, Adrianna."

***

His mouth came down hard on my lips, and the last thing I saw in the flickering firelight was the shadow of outstretched wings. Soot-colored feathers embraced me, and my feet no longer touched the floor.

Held tightly against his chest, I couldn't fight, and with his mouth pressing urgently against mine, I couldn't scream. It wouldn't have mattered. After all, I'd been warned.

No one can hear you in Hell.

Epilogue

I never saw the billions of damned souls he talked of, and I never caught a glimpse of Heaven. When he wished, we lived in his chambers in the House of Hades: magnificent, opulent, and dark. Most of the time, however, we were in the scriptorium—as he facetiously called it (because there was nothing remotely monastic there)—where I remade the books I'd ruined, and he worked on his own. Sometimes, he approved of my work. Many times, he did not.

Every year, as midsummer approached, he asked if I had finished. A thousand times, I said, "Not yet." And then I'd ask him, "Are you opening the shop?"

"No," he would answer, "I have no books to sell."

Then, shortly after the thousandth summer had passed, he entered the workroom. "I cannot keep you here any longer," he said, examining the few books that remained. "I have been . . . reminded by the power and glory that is my Father . . . that you have an unfinished life and a soul that are not mine—and may never be mine."

I started to protest, but he paused in his work and pressed his lips to my forehead. "It is only by His grace and your compassion that we have been allowed to stay together this long. Remember, Adrianna, I told you. There are no miracles or happy endings for spirits outside Heaven. You must go. I cannot and will not allow you to be undeservedly condemned to exile with an outcast for eternity."

We finished the books together and returned.

***

I carefully handed "Aidan" the last of one thousand new books—eight hundred and seventy that I remade, and one hundred and thirty of his own creation—and he set them, one at a time, on the newly polished shelves.

When he finished making sure they were perfectly aligned with the light, we hesitated at the doorway for a moment, then he firmly closed the door. "I'm not taking any more chances," he said, adding a larger "Do Not Enter" sign on the wall and sliding the steel bolt into the new latch at the top of the door.

"Why have a door here at all?"

"Because, when I'm in the shop alone, I like to come back here and, well, just look at them. Sometimes for pleasure or trying to decide which books should be next, or—"

"Or, perhaps, to be a little closer to Heaven?"

All expression left his face. "Perhaps."

I glanced up at the clock above the door; it still read 12:45.

"How did you turn the clock back?"

"*I* didn't," he said. "It was a gift."

"I'm grateful," I said softly.

I took a deep breath and tried to ask casually, "Will I see you next year?"

"I will never be here again, if that is what you are asking. It would be, shall I say, too tempting. I'm quite sure I would not be able to leave you twice."

"Can you tell me where you will be?"

"No. It's not that I can't; it's that I will not have you spend the rest of your life looking for me."

"Don't you ever want to see me again?"

"Oh, my Adrianna, I will see you . . . and sometimes you will see me."

"Will I know you?"

"No. I cannot interfere with the life you have here."

I felt myself smiling. "No more than you already have, you mean."

He looked at me solemnly. "One might say you interfered with mine."

I nodded, and although I could feel my heart breaking, I wondered at the lack of tears or sadness. I looked up at him with clear eyes. "Why am I not crying?"

"Because while your soul is standing on the edge of anticipation somewhere between despair and hope, your heart knows this is not the end," he said.

We walked to the front of the bookshop hand in hand. We did not speak. We did not think about the gleaming books in the locked room, each in its own place, leatherbound and gilt-edged, perfect and waiting. We ignored the coffee and tea display, all shiny and new, the chocolate biscotti standing upright like spears in the jar.

At twelve-fifty, he removed the key and a small package from his pocket. He unwrapped it, and I noticed the title had been scraped off the red leather cover. It was the book I'd damaged and, therefore, being no longer perfect, was forever unworthy of rooms radiant with rainbow light.

"Here is your book, Helena. Paid in full."

"After a thousand years, you remembered."

"I am incapable of forgetting one moment of you."

I reached for the book, but he held onto it.

"Choose to be good," he said. "I want to hear your voice again."

I nodded, and he released the book into my hands.

He inserted the key into the lock. I stood next to him and, putting my hand on his, stared into the unending depth of his eyes. We looked at each other in silence. Everything in the bookshop was so normal, so, so sane. For a moment, it seemed that everything that had occurred since I entered the bookshop had been my imagination. Surely, nothing like that would have ever *really* happened to me. I shook my head in wonder and remembrance.

"It was real, wasn't it?"

He smiled. Suddenly, Aidan crumpled to the floor. Before me, in the overly human setting of the perfect bookstore, he stood under the skylights, shining like a dark star. In some cultures, I learned, he was considered a god; in others, an archangel; and, in still others, a devil. Although they were all correct, he was none of these to me, for I did not worship his beauty or fear his power.

He reached for my hand.

"I could do that. I could tell you that you spilled your tea, slipped, and hit your head. I could spin a tale that would persuade you that everything you've experienced was a dream, a nightmare, or a hallucination. And, as your appearance has not altered, you would believe me because if everything we experienced together were true, surely it would have changed you in some way." He nodded to himself and continued, "Yes, I could do that, Adrianna, but I will not, for then you would begin to question, to doubt, and soon believe all you remembered, perhaps even cherished, was mere fantasy."

Gently taking my face in his hands, he looked into my eyes. "It would be less painful for both of us, but I will not let you think our time together was an illusion, that the feelings we share are not real, and that the last thousand years of my existence meant nothing more to you than a charade or a play of shadow puppets on a wall." He slipped a chain holding my gold ring over my head and kissed me. "I am not so easily dismissed, Adrianna. For dreams fade, images blur and are forgotten, but I will not allow that, for if I cannot forget a single moment, neither shall you." He pulled me to him as the black feathery curtain of his wings encircled me, and his hands moved over my body with the casual intimacy of a husband. I wanted time to stop—but Earth time does not stop.

The minutes ticked by, and I knew our time together was coming to an end. I could feel him drawing away, and when I looked up, he was once again Aidan.

The chime of the clock echoed in the silent room. As I turned toward the door, he touched my hair and whispered, "I forgive you, Adrianna."

"Truly?"

"Yes. Pray for me?"

"Always," I said.

He unlocked the door, and I stepped back into the Earth world.

Without another word, the door closed behind me. I stood motionless on the sidewalk. The storefront across the street reflected an image I hadn't seen in a millennium. My hair was the same length, my clothes fell around me as they always had, my lunch was as fresh as when I bought it, and my shoes—still slightly scuffed—fit perfectly. Everything visible about me was the same.

And everything about me was different.

The central Florida sun shone down on me like a stranger. Standing in its bright heat, my thoughts traveled to the man standing on the other side of the door in the growing darkness. Alone. I felt a scream building in my throat as I turned to grasp the doorknob, but I was too late. At my touch, the brass crumbled in my hand, the door faded into stucco-covered concrete, and the rusty mailbox was red dust before it touched the ground. A feeling of unrelenting despair swept over me. Invisible feathers brushed against my cheek, and I tasted smoke in the air. Like a sigh, I felt my body rise and then resettle gently on the sidewalk.

He was gone. The scream in my throat broke through as a strangled cry of farewell.

I looked down at the book in my hands and saw something protruding from the pages. I opened it to find a single black feather.

"I will be good," I promised.

I looked up the street toward my office, unchanged and waiting for my return. I glanced to my right and my left. I began walking.

"We make our own heaven," he'd once said to me, "and we make our own hell."

He was not wrong.

Afterword

Tonight, I am restless and beset by memories, so I have once again taken up my pen . . .

Of all the changes he made in my life, setting it on a different trajectory was the least of them. My focus and training now revolved around books, and, hoping to recreate even a small piece of paradise, I found work repairing ancient volumes in the rare book room at the Library of Congress. I'm a "wonder," they say, at restoration. When my colleagues ask where I learned such delicate precision, I tell them I was apprenticed to a master bookbinder in an Italian scriptorium. I'm not sure they believe me, but they rarely ask a second question.

Midsummers have come and gone, and while I have felt his presence over the years, I haven't seen him—not even once—and I have ceased looking for him. That he still looks for me is enough. Sometimes, I speculate where the portal is located: in a janitor's closet perhaps, at the top of the elevator shaft, or behind a mirror that isn't a mirror. On nights like this, I imagine him gliding past the shelves and stacks, his beauty lost in the darkness, calmly examining the titles of books in the largest library in the world.

The black feather wasn't the only remembrance he left tucked into my book. The other was a handwritten poem. Unsure of whether it is a promise or a prayer, I have encased them together in a gold frame, and deep inside—hidden from those who would never understand—is a small ring created from two gold wires, one wrapped around the other like ivy coiled around the trunk of a tree.

That frame sits on the small desk next to my bed atop a nameless book bound in red leather. Safe behind unbreakable glass and written in liquid gold, the words on the handmade paper gleam softly in the moonlight.

The poem reads:

Some stars fall
they crash—
fiery orbs of dying light,
Some stars rise
from ash—
forgiven and newly bright.
When I am
reborn—
by Divine mercy and might,
I'll find you
at dawn—
on wings of unbroken flight.

I was surprised that he wrote these words in English because he taught me Italian, as well as French and Spanish. I can also read and write Latin and Greek, but I never learned to speak either of them well. During our time in the scriptorium, we recreated books written by hundreds of talented men and women, as well as philosophers and fools, statesmen, heroes, poets, and martyrs. Our limitless discussions included art, design, literature, film, economics, the definition and impossibility of a just war, how the human world works, and why it will inevitably end.

But beyond all this, I learned there is a reason, as irrefutable as faith, why we were given this imperfect world, and despite those imperfections, I am reminded every minute of every day how much we will lose if we cannot work together with love and joy to bring Heaven to Earth."

And, because some things are too precious or painful to forget, I must add these last few lines.

I never held my daughters; my sons were taken from my arms. Their father, Aastéri-Katávasi (in Greek, or Lucifer in Latin, or Helél in Hebrew), would only tell me they were safe. I comforted myself with the slim hope of perhaps meeting their spirits someday, either in this life or the next. So, you see, our love gained me nothing but knowledge. All the children I thought I would never have seemed as lost to me as though I had never born them. It has been a long time, but I can still hear Aastéri's voice saying, "Amore mio, ogni scelta ha il suo prezzo." (My love, every choice has its price.)

And so, as I once said of him, the books became my children. I created them as lovingly as I could, perfect and golden. We spent centuries hidden away in the scriptorium, refining my composition skills as we made books for Heaven in his secret paradise on the borderlands of Hell.

Just before I left the scriptorium for the last time, he took my hand and led me to the dark room so that I could reclaim my human form and the steel-lined box. There, sheltered in the curve of my inert body, I saw our children snuggled together in a small nest of shredded linen, all sleeping as newborn babies will, their souls intact, their bodies never aging. My children: beautiful, warm, and alive.

"I will bring them with me," he promised, "and we shall have our days of glory."

Walking away from them was harder than leaving him, which is why, in his mercy, he waited until our last moments together to gift me with the knowledge of their existence to banish my despair and give me hope.

You may be wondering—if all I've written is true—why I didn't step in front of an oncoming bus or jump off the nearest bridge the afternoon he left me alone on the sidewalk. It is because if Aastéri wanted me dead, he would have killed me himself. I know, because I am still alive, that this phase of my existence was meant to continue.

Curious and unafraid, I wake up every morning of this, my unfinished life, looking forward to whatever opportunity, challenge, pain, or laughter comes next. As he advised, I continue to explore the avenues where the knowledge and insights I have acquired may take me, the doors my skills may open, and the good I can do in the world—in whatever shape or form that may take.

And tomorrow, as I do every day, I shall go to church and pray for Aastéri's living soul.

Now, however, Earth time weighs heavily on me, so I shall lay down my pen that I may sleep and dream of the laughter of our children and the days of glory that I know will surely come.

La Fine

Such Sweet Sorrow

"Good night, good night! Parting is such sweet sorrow,
That I shall say good night till it be morrow."
– William Shakespeare

Such Sweet Sorrow

It's been a long time coming, but I've decided to end it. For a few moments, all the break-up songs on the soundtrack of my life, from "Maggie May" to "Nothing Compares 2 U," echo in the back of my mind with dozens of others. I let the lyrics run out in full measure because tonight they are not simply popular songs about losing one's beloved. No, the relevance of these words lies in the fact that I am terminating a relationship I have cherished far longer than I have known those loved ones who are safely sleeping upstairs. This affair embraces a desire that exists in the very air I breathe, and has been as close to me as my fingertips, for nearly thirty years.

Despite my constant dedication, our alliance, as it were, has always been a precarious association. The slow seduction began when I was a child, watching and learning from the adults in my life, then grew into a kind of curious hunger as a teenager. A hunger I have succumbed to too many times against my better judgment—almost against my will—but I cannot call the satisfaction of such passion "nonconsensual." Even when compelled to beg, borrow, steal, or barter to answer the yearning of my body and soul, I initiated every encounter. The decades have passed, yet the urgency in my hands has never slowed; the excitement of anticipation has never faded. Regrettably, however, my original fascination with pursuing this pastime has slowly dwindled due to its resulting social isolation and medical revelations. I've begun to care more about longevity than longing, so I can no longer postpone the inevitable. In spite of my unabated craving, the time has come to sever this increasingly toxic relationship from my life.

Sitting alone in a room illuminated by moonlight streaming through blinds and sliced into layers against the wall, the setting seems strangely ceremonial, as though I were performing a dark rite. And perhaps I am, for this is the sanctuary in which I have chosen to smoke my last cigarette.

I have purposely selected this day. It is not a birthday, or a holiday, or a specific time of year for forgiveness or new beginnings. It is just a random day that I will not mark with an anniversary or a memorial; one that will, gradually, fade into my past with other miscellaneous days. This chosen night is perfect. It is clear, unclouded, and no rain falls to blur the world outside or encourage second thoughts.

I do not tread this ground lightly. It is a serious business, saving your own life. Yet, many have gone knowingly to their graves for the sake of these tightly wrapped chambers of death. I do not wish to be one of them, so I am willingly saying goodbye on my own terms—and my own turf—while I still can.

I have decided to stage my farewell scene on the lanai because it is not quite the house where the fumes and chemicals can creep into the crevices and carpets where my children play. Nor is it quite the outdoors, where everything looks dead in the darkness. The overhanging branches of the trees cast shadows on the ground that wave and shudder, and I am beset by memories, unbidden perhaps, but necessary to underscore the genesis of a commitment I thought would last forever.

Our love affair, rather one-sided but real nonetheless, started the summer I was fifteen when we were introduced by my cousin's cousin—sixteen, tall, and tan—who had "borrowed" two cigarettes from my aunt's purse. Sneaking out and meeting up behind the garage, he handed me one and lit a match on the bottom of his shoe. Despite my attempts to act cool, he had to light match after match as I puffed, coughed, and kept losing the burning end. I thought I had managed it fairly well and got halfway through the ordeal before I became ill. Still, even while I was bent over, hacking both my lungs and lunch out, I could not forget the feel of the delicate cylinder between my fingers and how naturally my lips pressed against the filter as the hot, sweet smoke filled my mouth and slid sinuously down my throat.

A moment later, my head was throbbing, and my throat was burning. I threw what was left of the cigarette on the ground and returned to the house. Upset in mind and body, I vowed never to do it again.

The next day, he stopped by my aunt's house again. Smiling teasingly, he pointed to the unmistakable bulge of two cigarettes in the pocket of his t-shirt. His slightly lifted eyebrows telegraphed a secret and a question.

"No," I said firmly.

The teasing look lingered in his eyes as he smiled and nodded. Watching him turn to leave the room, I whispered, "Yes."

He paused just for a moment between steps, and I ran to catch up with him and grasped his hand.

Delighted with these first few steps into the magical freedom of being an adult, it only took a few days before I was stealing my own. Every adult I knew smoked, and I never let an unattended pack go unmolested. I rarely smoked alone, and what had begun behind the garage was eventually finished in the backseat of my uncle's Lincoln Continental. We smoked there, too. Satiated with all things forbidden.

When I returned home after my summer of adult enlightenment, I found friends with older siblings who were quite willing—for a price, of course—to buy me a pack at a time. Cologne, mints, gum, and room deodorizer became my accomplices. I perfected lies and alibis for the inevitable confrontations from suspicious adults whose motto was "Don't do as I do, do as I say do."

In my only defense, I will say that I never encouraged anyone else to smoke. More out of selfishness than goodwill, of course. I just wasn't willing to share.

Since every affair has a beginning, I must be allowed to describe mine. Memories of that summer still make me smile. You never forget your first time.

Tonight, I feel free to entertain such memories as I have waited until everyone has fallen asleep. This is my time. I do not require an audience, a second opinion, an accolade, or someone to hold my hand. Sitting alone, my struggle is between the small, gleaming box that holds the heart of my addiction and all the awareness a surgeon general can impart. Regardless, I still feel the need to hold it, caress its length, slide the pristine white edge of the filter between my lips, and inhale its strength. I know it's waiting in its own dark room, sensually indolent with no will of its own, no light until I bring my fire, no life until I give it breath.

Slowly, as though I have all night, I lift the box to my forehead in a gesture of obeisance for everything each one of its inhabitants has meant to me: a friend, comforter, loyal companion, and yes, even a secret lover on lonely nights when the only warmth in my cold bed was the smoke rising, twisting, and yes, embracing me with fragrant heat. It would be impolite—almost disrespectful—to hasten the departure of such pleasant and patient company.

To mark the solemnity of the occasion, I hesitate before flipping open the carton's lid. Instead, I treat my senses to the beauty of a lingering farewell. Waving the box slowly, I take a moment to enjoy the aromatic mixture of tobacco and freshly bleached tree pulp. Pungent and sweet, these scents are as familiar to me as my favorite perfume. In the silence of the night, my ear catches the sound of the solitary item rolling between those smooth antiseptic walls, triggering a slow smile of pleasure at the knowledge that it is still there, still waiting. Seeking a calm moment while the rush of anticipation floods my brain, I find myself considering the irony of loving something that, while desperately needing my breath to fulfill its destiny, only wants to destroy me.

I try to push such dispiriting thoughts into the recesses of my mind, but they seem to resist, taunting me and applauding me by turns.

Unable to delay any further, I take the box in my right hand. Flipping the top backward with a single movement, I can't help but admire the luxury of the silver foil. The unexpected elegance makes me wonder (for the fiftieth—or five-hundredth—time) if it was done on purpose; juxtaposing a silver lining to instill a bit of hope and banish the inevitable dark cloud of reality.

Angling the moonlight into the shadowy corners of the only home it has ever known, I see the last slender resident waiting patiently. Snug in the corner, it shimmers in the light, dangerously silent and confident that it will not be alone forever. I shake the pack for the final time and let it tumble into my left hand.

My first instinct is to crush the cellophane-protected cardstock in my fist as a gesture of defiance, but I stop my fingers from tightening around the sharp folds. Pressing the foil deep into the container, I close it respectfully as one might lower the lid on a coffin and drop it unspoiled and shining into the wastebasket.

A familiar fragrance drifts upward as the thin white line slides seductively across my palm and comes to rest against my middle finger. Secure in my obsession and desire, if it were a man, he would wink knowingly and tip his hat; if it were a woman, she would arch her back in welcome. That it is neither male nor female is irrelevant to the intimacy we share.

Bidding a reluctant farewell to my first love, I lightly caress the crisp, pristine paper and appreciate the aroma of the chemically enhanced tobacco. Giving in to my fantasies, I hold it, unlit, between my fingers, toss my hair back, and pose like a glamourous movie star, pouty expression and all. The "cover girl" silhouette on the wall makes me laugh.

Since I know I will never do this again, I decide to go old school. Opening the drawer of the small table next to me, I take out the matches I use to light the candles that disguise the unmistakable smell of smoke. I scratch a match across the red emery of the matchbox, and although there is not a draft of wind in the room, I cup my hands around the small fire and carefully guide the flame to my last cigarette.

It is impossible to control my craving as I rush to inhale deeply. And, as ever, I instantly repent my greed. The deep hacking cough that has become all too frequent rumbles up from my chest and temporarily ruins the sensuality of the moment. Resentful that, once again, our relationship has cast me back to the beginning, where every puff ended in coughing spasms, I stare at the burning ember suspended between my fingers and wish I had the power to crush it out. Just crush it now and for all eternity . . . but I don't. Even as the smoke burns its way down my throat, desire burns through my mind, and I know it's impossible. It's the last one, our last time, and I won't let it go so quickly. Acknowledging my weakness, I slowly convey the moist end to my lips.

Taking it now with long, drawn-out sighs that gently fill my lungs with fragrant poison, I close my eyes and let the nicotine penetrate my consciousness. Dopamine surges through the pleasure centers of my brain, and I cannot stop a smile of pure joy as I bring the slowly darkening filter to my mouth again and again.

Leaning my head back on the cushions, I blow a few smoke rings through the beams of moonlight for old times' sake and remember the night my best friend taught me how to do that under the stadium bleachers. We had almost gotten caught, but it was dark then, too, and we weren't the only ones running toward the parking lot, still clutching the contraband tightly in our fists.

I watch as the smoke rings drift into memory and refocus on the subject at hand. Once costing less than two dollars a pack, the still-perfect box in the trash costs almost nine dollars. For a few minutes, I estimate how much money has literally gone up in smoke. Allowing one pack a day—and I know in my heart it was usually more—is three hundred and sixty-five packs a year; one year of smoking, at current prices, is about three thousand dollars. Times what? Ten? Fifteen? Twenty? Yes, even with subtracting the two years I didn't smoke while I was pregnant, my heart sinks when I imagine all the things we could do if I had that money right now. With numbers still running through my mind, I make yet another devastating calculation and stare in amazement at the seven-thousand, three-hundredth cigarette I've smoked in the last year. Dread fills my heart when I realize that much of the haze from the previous seven thousand two hundred ninety-nine cigarettes has infiltrated our children's perfect lungs as well as those of all the people I love.

Guilt over the true cost of my addiction washes over me and is sobering enough, but time and fire move tangentially, and I'm not sure if I regret the cost and the danger as much as my awareness that the slow burn has eaten its way toward my fingers with each warm mouthful of mortality until nothing is left but the filter.

I take my last lingering kiss, then farewell. This one-sided love affair is over.

Linda Ronstadt's voice echoes in my mind with the chorus to "You're No Good," as I press the filter firmly, almost resentfully, against the crystal dish I've always used as an ashtray, extinguishing its danger to me or anyone else. The snowy paper destroyed, the lovely sweetness used up; and, in the charred and twisted end, I see a death mask smiling ghastly in plain sight.

A sudden awareness sweeps over me. They knew. They always knew. Blinded by the irresistibility, bliss, and expectancy of the next and the next and the next, I failed to recognize the ugliness beyond the professionally marketed exterior or hear the silent laughter of tobacco chemists that followed every snap of the cellophane ribbon as I opened each new pack. Jolted by this new understanding, my mind goes back to my earlier thoughts, and I realize it was always about the money. Despite the manufactured enjoyment, the feel, the taste, and the longing for more that cigarettes gave me, it was strictly a cash-only arrangement— nothing more than immediate gratification for a price—and I was a dupe, just another "john" participating in the oldest profession in the world.

Apparently, one is never too old to feel foolish. Betrayed by the indulgences of my body and the enslavement of my mind, my focus shifts to the floor above the lanai. The bedroom where my non-smoking, hard-working husband lies, sleeping uneasily because I am not beside him, and the two smaller rooms that hold a promise of something I never thought we would have: a family. What kind of example had I been setting for my daughters? Did I make smoking look "cool"? When would they have started sneaking cigarettes from my purse? Or, did the constantly filled ashtray on the back porch dim the allure of adulthood for them? Which path would they choose? My mother's heart filled with remorse and love for those lives entrusted into my care, and tears spilled onto my cheeks.

With a willpower of its own, my right hand sought a cigarette pack where none existed. I shook my head and glanced around. What will I do now? I saw the sewing basket my sister gave me for my birthday. It was still on the edge of the couch, untouched from the moment I opened it. She made baby blankets for the community hospital and wanted me to join her small group. My daughters wanted music lessons. Claire asked for piano, Katie asked for singing, and they both wanted to take ballet. And I could help. I knew how to read music, and I'm fond of dance, plus, I'll have the time and the money now. Then I remembered that Ethan wanted to refinish the basement as a rec room. Perhaps it could be a family project. Without a cigarette break dragging me away every fifteen minutes, I could spend more time with all of them! Bittersweet excitement filled my heart.

I walked over and closed the window, shutting out the moonlight with its shadows of the past. On my way to the kitchen, I picked up the crystal dish and, looking beyond the smudges and ash, noticed the beauty of the engraved design. With hot, soapy water, I erased the evidence of a love affair so cleverly persuasive that I believed every word except those of warning.

Thinking of the next day, I decided to go slowly and ingratiate my newfound time and gratitude without fanfare or a big announcement. I knew the nicotine cravings would continue for months, maybe years, and that the battle would not be fought every day but every minute of every day until my brain got the message. I didn't want them worrying about me, watching me, or even encouraging me. It was my battle to fight, not theirs.

They are not my guardians; they are my family, and that is the only love affair that matters to me.

Drying the delicately etched glass, I watched the kitchen light catch the beveled edge and cast a rainbow against the kitchen wall. Too pretty to put away in a cabinet, I realized it would be an ideal dish for the girls' favorite candy.

Opening the pantry, I poured several heart-shaped chocolates wrapped in silver and red foil into the crystal bowl and brought it into the family room. After trying it in several different places, I set it on the bookshelf, where it will catch the morning sunlight and sparkle like a new day.

Adieu

Suggested Playlist

Song	_Recording Artist_
Wicked Game	Chris Isaak
In the Air Tonight	Phil Collins
Theme from Somewhere in Time	Roger Williams
My Immortal	Evanescence
Why	Annie Lennox
No More "I Love You's"	Annie Lennox
Viva La Vida	Coldplay
Djinn Theme	Tom Holkenborg
The Memory of Trees	Enya
A White Demon Love Song	The Killers
Home	Phillip Phillips
On My Way Home	Enya
Angel	Sarah McLachlan
Colors	Amos Lee
Firedance	Bill Whalen
Time after Time	Rod Stewart
I Will Find You	Clannad
Hope Has a Place	Enya
Until It's Time for You to Go	Neil Diamond
Hallelujah	Leonard Cohen
Only Time	Enya
Time Passages	Al Stewart
Time of the Season	Zombies
City of Angels	Gabriel Yared
From Where I Am	Enya
This Time	Jonathan Rhys Meyers
Start Again	Rob Simonsen and Faux Fix

Ordinary	Alex Warren
Time After Time	Mark Williams
Waiting for the Miracle	Leonard Cohen
Tea-House Moon	Enya
A Thousand Years	Christina Perri
Timeless and Free	Dan Gibson
We Have All the Time in the World	Royal Philharmonic Orchestra

Acknowledgements

To me, this book is more than a collection of short stories; it is a love letter to literature. An expression of gratitude to the University of Dayton mentors and professors in the English, History, and Religious Studies Departments, who believed that creative writing was not only a raison d'être but its greatest joy.

Not every writer has the advantage of the support, kindness, and assistance I have received since I began writing for publication almost fifteen years ago from my friends and family, as well as the professional writers and copy editors I have met along the way. I am grateful for each moment spent and every kind word said that have helped me navigate the path from proofreader to author.

For her invaluable assistance as critique partner, consultant, and cheerleader, I would like to thank Mary Lu Scholl, author and artist. I'm quite sure this book would still be in pieces on my computer if not for her expertise and unlimited patience.

I must also express my gratitude to Bryn Donovan, romance editor extraordinaire, Richard D. Cohen, scriptorium aficionado, and the wonderful authors of the Thursday Night Critique Group: Erica, Merry, Ryan, and Travis, for their insightful questions, suggestions, and unfailing support.

Last, but never least, I want to thank James, Debra, and Dale for their encouragement and for perfecting the art of "not rolling their eyes" while listening to my rambling stories.

Et Rémi, qui me rappelle chaque jour que même l'amour impossible dure pour toujours.

Thank you

I would like to thank you for reading *The Bookbinder's Apprentice and other Impossible Love Stories.* If you enjoyed it, please consider leaving a review on Goodreads and/or the bookseller from whom you purchased this collection.

I would also like to invite you to consider my other books – available on Amazon and wherever "impossible" love stories are sold.

About the Author

On the day she decided she wanted more than copyediting other writers' manuscripts, PJ began her transition from copy editor to author. Her debut novel, *The Fire Slayers*, blended science fiction with love and loyalty. In *Finding Persephone*, the intrigue and romance deepen when an alien assassin, charged with keeping the secrets of an underground brotherhood, risks losing everything when he falls in love. Her third novel in the series, *Persephone's Children*, takes all those genres a step further when the alien brotherhood threatens the life of the woman he loves and the children he has sworn to protect.

In *The Bookbinder's Apprentice and other Impossible Love Stories*, PJ stretches the romance genre into new territory, including paranormal, history, and fantasy.

When PJ isn't writing impossible love stories, you can find her sitting on the sun deck with her rescued Aussies, Nymeria and Kaela. She will be the one with a book in one hand and a glass of sangria in the other.

Read more about her work:
- http://pjbraley.com/ • @pjbraley.bsky.social
- https://www.facebook.com/PJBraleyAuthor